STOLEN

Everyday Heroes Series Book Five

Margaret Daley

Stolen
Copyright © 2019 by Margaret Daley

I'm dedicating this book to
Abbey and Aubrey.

My appreciation:
I want to thank Aubrey for her patience and
persistence in taking the photo
of the dog on the cover.

ONE

At eight-thirty Thursday morning, Cimarron City Detective Nick Davidson, the lead on the new case, and his partner, Brad Thomas, approached the crime scene, a one-story, red-bricked house. Nick scanned the street, noting a few people watching them from nearby yards or porches. Had one of them seen something that would help him solve the crime he was sent to investigate? He hoped so.

Nick nodded to the officer standing guard at the door. "Where's Officer Brown?" He put on his latex gloves.

"He's at the back door." Officer Nelson gestured toward in that direction. "The victim, Mary Phillips, is in the kitchen. She was stabbed numerous times with probably a butcher knife. We couldn't find the murder weapon. The medical examiner was called, and the scene is secured. We didn't find another body. Other than the blood trail, the living and dining rooms and the kitchen were clean and orderly, but the master bedroom and the one across the hall were ransacked. The third bedroom wasn't touched that we can tell."

"Thanks." Nick signed the log, waited for Brad to do the same, then opened the screen door. Concealed from view except for a couple of neighbors directly across the street, the front door had been breached by the murderer. Nick examined it. The intruder had kicked it in. There wasn't a doorbell with a camera, so he couldn't pull footage from it. He took pictures of the damage, hoping there were cameras inside.

After moving into the foyer, Nick turned to his partner. "I know the officers have gone through the house, but check it again while I follow the blood trail."

Brad nodded. "Will do."

While Nick headed right, his partner went left. Nick made his way through the living and dining rooms, following the red drops into the kitchen while taking photos as he went. He'd been a detective with the CCPD for six years and had been to numerous murders, but he still wasn't immune to the violence. And never would be. It reinforced why he'd become a police officer.

From the primary information he'd received on his way here, a young woman had been stabbed multiple times while fleeing from an intruder. A neighbor saw a man jumping over the rear fence. The lady next door called Mary Phillips, but when she hadn't answered, the neighbor called 9-1-1.

When Nick entered the kitchen, Officer Brown stood by the back door. Nick scanned the room, noting the island in the center blocking his full view of the scene. His gaze fixed upon an arcing spray of blood on the counter and cabinets near the refrigerator. The odor of death filled his nostrils while his heart pounded against his ribcage. He walked around the island and came to a halt several feet away from the body of a woman, face down in a pool of blood, smears of it on the tile floor as if she'd tried to crawl away from the killer.

"Are the crime scene techs on the way?" Nick put his fingers against her neck to feel for a pulse. There wasn't any sign of life, but that was what he had expected.

"Yes." Officer Brown kept his gaze

focused straight ahead, away from the dead body.

The young cop's face had a gray cast to it. In the ten years Nick had been a police officer, he remembered his own struggles dealing with violent crime scenes. "Is this your first murder?"

"Yes, sir."

As Nick took a series of photos of the victim, a metallic taste coated his mouth. "Focus on the fact that we're going to find her murderer." After documenting the four knife wounds on the victim's back—none of which would have been deep enough to cause her death–he gently turned her over. When his gaze locked on hers, he swallowed hard. Cloudy blue, lifeless eyes stared at him.

Nick tore his attention from her face and let it sweep down her body. He found several defensive cuts, but the fatal stab wound had been into her heart. It looked like she first encountered the killer in her living room entrance and fled toward the rear of the house, which accounted for the slashes on her back. But in the kitchen, she must have turned toward the assailant. Why didn't she keep going toward the door that led outside? Was there more than one intruder who blocked her escape? A lot of questions and few answers.

"I understand Officer Nelson said there wasn't a sign of a murder weapon—a large butcher knife most likely. Is that right?" Nick asked as he continued to document the crime scene with pictures and notes.

"Yes. I checked for the weapon in the knife block on the counter and in the utensil drawer. There was no trace of blood on any of them."

So, possibly, the murderer brought his own weapon, or he used a knife from here, wiped it clean, and put it back into place. The crime scene techs would examine each knife in the house. Nick needed to check the house thoroughly as he expanded his search outward from the body. After taking his close-up photos and jotting down notes on what he saw, Nick stood and began his survey of the area around the victim before working his way outward. He'd found murder weapons in myriad places like under the floorboards, in a wall, in light fixtures, taped to furniture, in a toilet tank, and many other spaces.

On the counter, he found Mary Phillips's purse and carefully withdrew each item. He flipped through the photos in her wallet and found various pictures of a little girl with blond hair and blue eyes similar to the victim. Probably her child. If so, where was she? At a friend's? Taken by the killer? Nick checked the clock on the wall. Nine o'clock. This was fall break, the time that allowed the teachers to go to their state convention, so being at school wasn't a possibility. Unless she was visiting overnight with a friend or relative, the little girl should have been at home.

His investigation quickly shifted to include finding a missing child. He called his partner, who was going through the bedrooms. "Have you found a child's room?"

"I'm standing in it. From the frills, pink walls, and dolls, I'd say it belongs to a young girl. It's a mess as Officer Nelson said."

"A top priority will be finding the child." After he talked with Brad, he called the station and let his captain know about the missing girl. "I need someone there to research what they can about Mary Phillips. I went through her wallet, and she has several photos of a little girl about five or six. If I can get into her cell phone and find a good picture of the child, I'll send it to you right away so you can send out an Amber Alert if needed. I'll search for anything here that will help us find her."

When Nick disconnected his call, he picked up a cell phone on the counter near the victim's purse and clicked it on. He didn't expect it would open up for him to search, but a fingerprint would probably allow him in. He walked back to Mary Phillips, lifted her hand to place a finger on the screen, and gained access. He first went through the photos, found several recent ones of the little girl, and sent them to his e-mail address and the police department. Then he went through the phone and jotted down any information he thought might help him to solve the victim's murder. Next, he scoured through her current e-mails and texts for any help finding people connected to the family who could assist with finding the child, and he jotted their names down. Some of them he knew through his church. He also skimmed for any threatening messages. None. But he'd give her computer and cell phone to tech support to check for deleted e-mails, texts, and anything else that would help solve this case.

As he finished his search of Mary Phillips's phone, the medical examiner and crime scene technicians came into the kitchen. Nick finished his search of the room and made sketches and notes of the scene, taking photos from all angles.

When his partner entered the kitchen, Nick headed outside, eager to talk with the neighbors as well as follow up on a man seen jumping over the back fence. His captain had said he would deal with the missing child possibility while Nick worked the murder crime scene. He would process the scene and comb the neighborhood for answers, but he couldn't get it out of his head that a little girl could have been kidnapped. It reminded him painfully about his best friend in elementary school who'd been abducted coming home from school. Ben was never found, and Nick wouldn't ever forget that. The memory provoked all the feelings, from anger through to grief, that he'd processed over the years.

He walked up to the house on the left of the lady who called 9-1-1. Nick hadn't heard back from headquarters yet about where the victim's daughter might be. An urgency gripped him. A little girl's life might be at stake, and he was determined to find her as well as her mother's killer.

* * *

Dr. Sarah Collins rose from her chair as her patient stood. "I'm glad to hear you're getting a lot out of the survivor's group. Continue to exercise and write your thoughts down in your journal. You need a way to vent your anger and stress. Facing death and surviving isn't easy. The feelings you've experienced shouldn't be suppressed. The bombings we had several months ago affected a lot of people in Cimarron City. Nancy, you're progressing. It will take time. Have you decided to get a dog or cat? Pets can comfort people who are anxious and tense."

Nancy grinned. "A cat. A friend has one that gave birth to a litter of six. I'm taking two of them when they're big enough to be separated from their mother. Hopefully I'll be able to pick them up soon. Now I just have to convince my husband it's a good idea. Mark isn't keen on having a pet, but," she shrugged, "he doesn't think I need a therapist either."

Sarah walked with Nancy Byrd to the exit. "I'm glad to see you're acting on my suggestion. I hope it works out for you." Her patient left through the private side door. Someone rapped on her main one. "Come in."

Her secretary, Allie Johnson, entered. "Your next client, Nate Sommers, has canceled. He called to let you know he's sick."

"Thank you. It'll give me time to catch up on my notes." Sarah hated Nate missing an appointment. He was dealing with a lot of anxiety from the death of his child. She would call and check in on him.

Allie remained. "There's another problem. I just got an Amber Alert on my phone for Mary Phillips's daughter."

One of her patients. "Oh, no. I'm surprised I haven't heard from her." Sarah crossed to her desk, grabbed her purse in the bottom drawer, and withdrew it. "I'm going over to Mary's house. If she needs me, I may rearrange some of my other clients scheduled today." She hoped it had nothing to do with Mary's ex-husband finding them and kidnapping Candy.

Sarah hurried toward the private entrance into her office, swung the door open, and stepped out into a side hallway. She nearly stumbled over a bouquet of pink carnations in the middle of the exit. She clutched the doorframe to keep herself upright. Her heartbeat increased. No card had been left with the gift. This was the second flower arrangement from an unknown person she'd received in the last two weeks. She hadn't been concerned with the first one because occasionally a client would give her a present as a thank you. But for the time being, she couldn't think about the mysterious bouquet of carnations, her favorite flower. Mary might need her.

After quickly putting the vase on a cabinet near the door, she continued her trek to her car in the parking lot. She slipped into her red Chevy and placed a call to Mary. No one answered. Mary had to be distraught over Candy's disappearance, especially if the child's father took her. She couldn't even begin to know what Mary was going through, but she intended to be there for her.

She started her engine, and a thought struck her. The flowers weren't there when Nancy left by the private entrance. Only a couple of minutes had passed when Sarah opened the door to leave her office. A shiver snaked up her spine. She just missed seeing whoever left the bouquet because normally she wouldn't be leaving right after a patient. She shook her head, trying to rid herself of all thoughts except that Mary might need her.

As Sarah drove from the parking lot, she

turned on the radio to see if she could get any information about Candy's disappearance. Two streets away from Mary's house, the news came on, alerting Sarah to the murder of her patient. She pulled over to the curb to digest the announcement. Dead. Murdered. Why? Who would kill her?

Her stomach knotted with the thought that Mary's ex-husband fulfilled his promise to her. He wanted to make her pay for what she did—filing charges against him for abuse and divorcing him—and to take his daughter away from Mary.

"If anyone has information concerning Candace Phillips, a six-year-old with long blond hair and blue eyes, please contact the police."

She was only a couple of blocks away. Should she go to the scene of the crime?

Yes.

She continued her trip to Mary's house. She had information that might help the police. And if what she knew could assist them to find Candy, she would help the best she could to find her murdered client's daughter.

When Sarah arrived on Mary's street, she parked several houses down from her patient's home because of the police vehicles. As she walked toward the crime scene, the sight of the yellow tape roping off the area around the place where Mary had been killed made the news of her death concrete. She'd hoped the news had been wrong.

Sarah slowed her steps. A lump lodged in her throat as she desperately tried to keep her emotions in check. She paused on the outskirts of a small crowd that had formed. Several people from church stood in the crowd, and one person was a patient of hers.

She paused next to Andrew Ford, who lived down the street from Mary. "Do you know what happened?"

"Not much other than what I heard on the radio. The police are still inside. They just took her body away. I've heard Candy's missing, and I'm here to help. A couple of the other neighbors and I want to start a search for Candy. We've got to do something."

"I agree. That's one of the reasons I'm here." She spied Detective Nick Davidson, a parishioner at the church she attended and a casual acquaintance. He lifted the yellow tape, and ducked under it. Andrew was timid and needed to be encouraged to do what he wanted. "Let the police know you're happy to help. Call the station and see what they're organizing."

Andrew nodded. "I will." He turned and walked away from her, pulling out his phone.

Sarah continued her trek toward Nick, her pace increasing as the seconds ticked away. His gaze swept the crowd. She waved toward him as he covered the distance between them. He signaled a uniform cop to let her through the barricade.

"Why are you here? Did you know Mary Phillips?"

"Yes, I knew her. She's a patient of mine. What happened to her daughter?" She'd find out the circumstances surrounding Mary's murder, but right now, Sarah's priority was finding Candy.

"She isn't at the house. Headquarters is getting calls from friends of Mary and Candy. No one has come forward to say she's with them, so at this point, we have to consider that the killer took Candy. Do you have any idea who would murder Mary and kidnap Candy?"

"Her ex-husband, Jack Coleman. He doesn't live here. She's worked hard to stay under the radar because he was a bully and liked to use Mary and even Candy as a punching bag. They escaped seventeen months ago with the help of a women's shelter. I've been working with Mary for the past sixteen months. She was doing well until the bomber struck. She was in the grocery store when it went off."

Nick ran his fingers through his short dark brown hair and kneaded his nape. "Do you know where Jack Coleman is?"

"Mary used to live in Houston. He might be there." Bits and pieces of her conversations with Mary popped into Sarah's mind—especially concerning how Mary was trying to protect herself and her daughter from her ex-husband. She'd cut all ties with Houston and lived under an assumed name. She was missing something important. She listened to so many patients in the course of a week. That was why her notes were so important to her.

"Sarah? Do you remember something?" Nick furrowed his brows and narrowed his gray eyes.

"I want to help you. Mary had a rough life. I want to make sure the person who killed her is caught and brought to justice. I feel like I'm missing something. I'm trying to think through what Mary's said to me over the past year. I have notes from her weekly sessions that I can go through and see if there's anything that might point to a person besides her ex-husband. That will take a while. Is it possible for me to walk through her house? Something might trigger my memory." She didn't think anyone would have a motive besides Jack Coleman.

"Not at the moment. My partner and I are interviewing the neighbors. The crime scene techs are still processing the house. After that I can go with you through the place, but it'll be at least an hour or two depending on what tips we get." He withdrew a card from his pocket and handed it to Sarah. "Call me if you come up with anything that can help. When I'm finished, I'll let you know. I appreciate any insight into Mary's life." Nick took another card from his pocket and handed it to her. "Write your phone number on the back of this card."

Sarah scribbled it down for him. "I'm going back to my office to start going through the notes from Mary's sessions." She couldn't stand around here doing nothing until Nick finished interviewing the neighbors. She hoped one of them saw something or the killer was caught on a security camera.

She walked with Nick as he headed toward a house next door on the right. When they parted ways, he went up the sidewalk to the home while she continued her trek to her car. She paused at the driver's side door and glanced at Mary's place. A vague memory niggled at her mind. Mary had been so excited about finding her house seven months ago because...

Why was Mary so energized about the house? She'd gotten a raise at work which had led her to the decision about buying a home. She hated living in an apartment.

Suddenly Sarah remembered. She hurried toward the neighbor's house where Nick was going. She might know where Candy was.

TWO

Nick descended the porch steps, discouraged that the next-door neighbor on the right hadn't seen or heard anything and the other one on the left only saw a glimpse of a large man going over the back fence. He'd hoped the lady who called 9-1-1 would have more information.

"Nick, wait."

He heard his name and turned toward the sound. Sarah headed toward him. Maybe she remembered something about Mary that might help him with the case. He met her on the sidewalk. The look on her face gave him hope.

She stopped next to him. "Did you find a hiding place in Mary's home?"

"No. When we go through a house, we

check under beds, behind couches, and anything like that."

"It's possible that Candy's in a secret hiding place." Sarah kept walking toward Mary's.

Nick clasped her arm and halted her progress. "What are you talking about? A secret place? No, we didn't find anything like that. Where is it?"

"Mary called it her safe room. It's in Mary's bedroom in the closet."

"My partner went through it and didn't find anything like that."

"Mary took what was already there and made it so she and Candy could go into it if there was any kind of trouble. She still lived in fear Jack Coleman would find her no matter where she went. I know the general location, but that's all."

Nick started for the victim's house, avoiding the crowd still out front that slowed their progress. The prospects that the child might still be at home lifted his spirits. "Why didn't the little girl come out when we got there?"

"Because her mother made it very clear to Candy not to come out until Mary said it was okay. Can I go inside with you? If Candy's in the hiding place, she'll need me.

She knows me."

He stopped and glanced over his shoulder. "Yes."

When Sarah joined him, he resumed his fast pace. "I hope she's in there."

"Me, too." When he went inside, he stopped in the foyer. "There's a trail of blood that starts in the living room and goes all the way into the kitchen where we found Mary's body. If we find Candy, and I pray we do, we have to keep the child from seeing it."

As they passed the entrance into the living room, the color drained from Sarah's face. A stray strand of her blond hair came loose from her bun, and she hooked it behind her ear while she averted her dark brown gaze and hurried her steps. "Can you cover that up if Candy's here?"

"I'll find a way, so she won't see it." *Lord, please let Candy be here*. When his best friend had been kidnapped, Nick was supposed to be with him walking home, but that day, he'd broken a tooth on the playground equipment, and his mother had taken him to the dentist after school. If he'd been there, maybe Ben might still be here today. He couldn't shake the feeling he was responsible no matter what others had said.

Nick paused in the entrance to Mary's bedroom and gestured toward the room across the hall. "As you can see, the killer ransacked these."

"But not the other rooms?"

"Right. Which makes me think this could be the work of Mary's ex-husband. It's possible he killed his ex-wife and took his daughter." He prayed he was wrong.

Sarah sucked in a deep breath then released it while shaking her head. "I agree. The ransacking could be him exhibiting his rage. If he has her, no telling what he'll do to Candy. The reason Mary finally got up the courage to leave him was because her husband began taking his anger out on Candy as well as Mary."

Anger surged through Nick as he balled his hands. His father had used him as a punching bag until Nick had grown up and been able to defend himself. The thought of hitting a little girl churned his stomach. "We've got to find her." He entered Mary's bedroom and picked his way through the rubble on the carpet.

Everything that could be smashed was lying on the floor in shattered bits. The covers had been yanked from the bed while the sheets, with bloodstains on them, had been torn in several places as if the killer had used the knife, he'd stabbed Mary with, to rip them and clean off the murder weapon.

"This was very personal." Sarah picked her way toward the big walk-in closet, the door standing wide open.

"Jack Coleman definitely had a motive if he found where his ex-wife relocated." He came up behind Sarah and glanced over her shoulder at the disarray. "Where do you think the secret place is? What would Mary do?"

Sarah moved forward, nearly falling when she stepped on a shoe.

Nick quickly grasped her and kept her from going down.

"Candy, this is Sarah Collins, Anna's mom. If you're in here, please come out. I'm here for your mom to help you."

Nick held his breath as he waited for a response. But silence greeted Sarah's plea. "Candy, you're safe now. I'm a police officer, here with Sarah. We want to help you." Still nothing. Nick scanned the ransacked closet, looking for anything that indicated a possible door to a hidden area.

Sarah waded through the clutter until she was at the back of the closet where there were shelves for shoes, all swept off the ledges. "Candy, if you're in here, we need to know you're all right. Please let us know." As she said those words, she felt around the shoe rack. "If this isn't it, I don't know where it is."

Nick looked up at the ceiling. Some closets had a way into the attic. But not in the victim's case, and it wouldn't have been a secret if there had been a door that could lead into a hidden room. When his gaze returned to Sarah, she stood on her tiptoes trying to feel the top of the shelving. Being five feet two or three inches, she couldn't. He closed the gap between them and ran his gaze and hand along the back of the ledge. Nothing.

Sarah knelt and inspected the bottom of the shoe rack about six inches off the floor. "I found it."

A click sounded, and the secret door slowly opened, stopping when shoes were blocking it from going all the way. Sarah swept the obtrusion away, and the panel kept moving.

Nick spied the little girl huddled into a ball, her back to him, her hands over her ears. His heart broke at the sight.

* * *

Sarah tried to draw in a decent breath, but she couldn't. Seeing Candy wrapped up in a ball of protection, clutching her big Teddy bear, made Sarah's lungs cry for air. She had to be strong for the child. She owed Mary that much. She knew what it was like to be abused, but in her case, it had been a boyfriend in high school, not a husband. Her parents had been there to support her once she'd told them what was going on.

Drawing in deep breaths, she managed to move around Nick and entered the small hidden room no more than four feet deep, six wide, and nine high, as though it had been part of the walk-in closet at one time. It would be big enough to fit both Mary and her daughter inside the safe room. "Candy, I'm here to help. The bad man's gone." While Nick stayed at the entrance, Sarah knelt and laid a hand on the child's hunched shoulder. "You're safe." For a long moment, the little girl remained silent until sobs began to fill the air. Sarah wrapped her arms as much as she could around the child. "The police are here to help."

Candy lifted her head and looked at Sarah, her arms around the bear held against her chest. "Where's Mom? I heard..." She dropped her gaze. "I heard—her scream." Her shoulders quaked as the tears flowed from her eyes.

"Honey, let's get out of here."

The little girl shook her head, her ponytail swinging. "Mom told me to stay here," she swallowed hard and glanced up at her, "until she came to get me. I have to wait here. I have to..." Her wavering voice faded into silence.

"She wanted me to get you and leave here. Anna can't wait to play with you. Maybe you can spend the night with us." Her daughter was a good friend. They were in the same class at school and Sunday school at church. As the child lifted her head again, Sarah brushed Candy's hair away from her face. "Your mother wants me to take care of you when she isn't around. I told her I would."

"Did he hurt Mom?" Her big blue eyes fixed on Sarah, fear and confusion battling for supremacy.

What had Candy seen earlier? Sarah glanced over her shoulder at Nick, still in the entrance, his jaws locked in a hard line. He nodded, letting her take over the questioning of Mary's daughter. "Who are you talking about? Who hurt your mom?"

The child hunched her shoulders while burying her face against her folded arms and the softness of her Teddy bear.

"Candy, it's important. Did you see a man in the house earlier?"

For a long moment, the little girl didn't say anything as she again curled into a ball, hiding her face against her stuffed animal. Silence ruled.

"I'm not leaving you. I'll be right outside." Sarah stood and left the small enclosure. When she emerged into the walk-in closet, she motioned for Nick to follow her into the bedroom. "I don't want her overhearing us talk," she whispered and took several more steps away from the child. "Three months ago, Mary asked me if I would take custody of Candy if anything happened to her. She wanted to make it legal that I would be her daughter's guardian. I signed the papers eight weeks ago. That should allow the authorities to let Candy remain with me until I can finalize a guardianship or adoption." Sarah had always wanted more children than Anna, but when Charlie died in a wreck caused by a drunk driver five years ago, that dream died with him. She never wanted to love a person that much again.

"Was she having a problem with anyone besides Jack Coleman?"

"Not that she told me as a friend and as her therapist. Her ex-husband got out of prison three months ago. That was what caused her to ask me, and I couldn't turn her down. My daughter and Candy have been getting really close. At school they're in the same class. Mary needed a safety net after all she'd gone through. Her ex-husband only went to jail for fourteen months for the abuse he inflicted on his wife and daughter."

"So, the primary suspect is Mary Phillips's ex-husband."

"If he discovered where Mary lived, he could be your main suspect."

"I'll contact authorities in Texas, especially Houston, about Jack Coleman and find his most recent whereabouts."

"Do it quietly. I don't want the man to know where Candy is. He lost his right to be her father when he put his daughter in the hospital with a broken leg and bruises all over her. That was what drove Mary to have the courage to leave him." Sarah scanned the ransacked bedroom. "It has to be him." She swept her arm across her body, indicating the mess. "As I said earlier, the ransacking indicates a lot of rage in the person who did it. He was looking for his child after killing his ex-wife. Why else would someone only go through Mary's and Candy's rooms after murdering Mary?"

"Good question. If this had been a robbery, then why didn't the intruder take Mary's purse that was sitting on the counter in the kitchen with her cell phone right next to it? She had two hundred dollars in her wallet. Her TV and laptop are still here."

Sarah looked back at the walk-in closet. "I'm going to try to persuade Candy to go home with me. She needs to be in a safe place."

"I agree. I'll stay out here. My presence might be worrying her. I've seen her at church, but I've never interacted with her."

"She's usually reserved and quiet except around Anna. My daughter will be good for Candy."

When Sarah returned to the hiding place, she found Candy standing up, leaning against the wall with the bear pressed against her chest. "Are you ready to go home with me? You'll be a nice surprise for Anna." Sarah held out her hand and prayed that Candy took it. Sarah wanted to get the child away from the scene of the crime.

For a long moment, the little girl stared at the hand offered to her. Sarah began to think Candy might not want to leave the "safe room" because in her mind this place had protected her. The outside world held the killer. When Sarah's boyfriend finally revealed his true self and beat her up, all she'd wanted to do was find a safe place and hide from the world.

Candy pushed off the wall and covered the short space between them. "Where's Mom? Did he hurt her?" The words of the last question quavered, ending in silence.

Sarah didn't want to answer the questions until they were away from the house. She was worried the child would try to find her mother. But looking into Candy's face, Sarah didn't have a choice. But not here where the sheets had been slit and tossed on the floor. "Let's talk in your spare bedroom."

Nick had apparently covered the torn, bloody sheets with a cover while waiting for Sarah and Candy to leave the safe room. Sarah released a long breath and gave Nick a slight nod. He fell into step slightly behind Sarah and Candy as they made their way to the only room not touched in some way by what happened today.

As Sarah entered the third bedroom, Nick caught her arm and leaned close to her ear, whispering, "I'll be out in the hall. After the house has been completely processed, I'll bring a couple of bags of Candy's belongings and clothes to your home. Later, you can come back and get everything else you'll need."

She smiled, the corners of her mouth quivering. "Thanks, especially about hiding the bloody sheets from Candy and packing a few things for her."

The little girl sat on the bed, folding her arms to keep her Teddy bear next to her chest like a shield of protection.

Sarah sat next to her. "There's no easy way to tell you this." She drew in a fortifying breath, her heart pounding against her ribcage. "Candy, your mother is dead. She's gone home to Heaven."

The little girl's head dropped forward, her chin resting against her bear. "Why did she leave me alone?"

"She didn't. She wanted me to look after you if anything happened to her. She didn't have a choice, honey. An intruder killed her." She hated having to say those words, but she didn't want Candy to think her mother abandoned her. "The police are dedicated to finding the person. How did you know to go to your safe room?"

A long silence fell between them.

Sarah slid her arm around Candy and waited for the child to speak.

"She screamed the safe word—Molly," the child mumbled against her stuffed animal.

"Molly? Your bear's name?"

Candy nodded and squeezed her Teddy bear tighter.

When Candy first came over to play with Anna, she used to bring Molly, but after a few visits, she began leaving it at home. She asked Mary about it. Candy felt safe coming over to their house and didn't need her stuffed animal anymore. That was when Mary had asked Sarah about being her daughter's guardian if anything happened to her.

"Where were you when she said Molly?" Sarah needed to get any information she could to help Nick find out who did this.

"In the hallway. I was going to the," Candy shuddered, "kitchen."

"Did you see anything?"

The color washed from the child's face. Tears filled her eyes and coursed down her cheeks.

"Honey, did you? I'm here to help. You're safe now."

Candy opened her mouth, but no words came out.

THREE

Hours later, Nick pulled up to Sarah's house. He wanted to check on Candy and see if the child recalled anything about what happened to her mother. Earlier, the little girl had clammed up when Sarah had asked if she'd seen anything. Most likely, there wasn't anything new because Sarah would have called to let him know. After canvassing the neighborhood with his partner, Nick realized they had little to go on. The few surveillance cameras on the street had been disabled during the night, leading Nick to realize that the killer had cased the area and taken out anything that could possibly identify him. This wasn't a spur of the moment decision to break into Mary Phillips's house and kill her. It had been planned and executed with the goal to keep the killer's identity a secret.

This had been a calculated murder. Everyone Nick had talked to in the neighborhood and at the International Foods, Inc., where Mary worked, only had good things to say about the woman. That reinforced his conjecture that the only person Nick could think would go to this length to kill Mary was her ex-husband. Nick was still waiting to hear back from the Houston police concerning Jack Coleman and his whereabouts because that man had a vendetta against his ex-wife from what Sarah told him and what the police records on Coleman indicated.

Nick mounted the steps to the porch and rang the bell. Seconds later, the door opened.

Sarah's half grin graced her mouth, her long blond hair hanging down rather than in the bun she wore earlier. "I saw you park in the driveway. Have you found the killer?"

For a few seconds, his attention was focused on how a smile could transform her. A light glittered in her dark brown eyes and momentarily transformed her face in the midst of this tragedy. "No," he finally answered and entered her house. "When I do, I'll inform you. I know how worried you are about Candy. How's she doing since you brought her to your house?"

"Quiet. She's with Anna in her bedroom."

"Has she said anything since you talked with her at her home?"

"No, but as I told you before we left, I think she knows something that may help you find the killer. When I questioned her about what she saw, she clammed up again. And since then, she's said little about anything. Candy's suppressed whatever she saw, which isn't surprising. What took place overwhelmed her. She may never be able to talk about it. But right now, my daughter is talking for both of them. I was on the way to the kitchen to make a snack for us. You're welcome to join us."

"Do you have any coffee?"

"Yes. I was going to make another pot. I drink way too much of it."

"So do I, but at the moment, I need to stay alert." Nick followed Sarah into the kitchen. "Where's your aunt?" He knew through church that Louise Morgan came to live with Sarah after her husband was killed in a car wreck.

"At the grocery store. She's buying food that Candy likes. I want to make this change as less stressful as possible. Later, when Aunt Louise returns, I'm going to my office to get my notes on Mary. With settling Candy into our house and fixing up the fourth bedroom for her, I haven't had the time. I still think it's Mary's ex-husband," Sarah said as she made a pot of coffee.

"He's number one on my short list. No one at work or in the neighborhood I interviewed could think of anyone who had a reason for murdering Mary. Call it a gut feeling. I'm beginning to rule out the possibility it was random the more I think about it. It has to be premeditated if he took out the cameras and brought his own weapon."

"The ransacked bedrooms make the crime feel personal, as though the person was looking for something, especially in a child's room. What does a six-year-old have that would be worth stealing? If I were a robber, that wouldn't be one of the first places I looked. If someone was searching for Candy, then that person would definitely check her bedroom. If that's the case, it has to be her father. Who else would be going after her?" Sarah raked her fingers through her hair, lines of frustration furrowing her forehead. "I can't think of anyone else."

"Another reason I have to take a hard look at Coleman. I hoped to get more information from the Houston Police Department and the parole officer assigned to him, especially if Coleman has lived there since he got out of prison." The scent of coffee percolating filled the room.

"Will you let me know what you find out? I have a good security system, and my aunt was in the military. She knows how to defend herself. I'm looking into putting up cameras as an added layer of protection. Mary had an alarm system but nothing else. She must have turned it off when she got up. She would have been leaving soon to go to IFI. She works from eight to five. IFI has a child-care facility for the employees to use long term or temporary. The company does something extra during school breaks when they have more kids to watch."

Nick pictured Louise Morgan teaching self-defense to women at their church. "Yeah, your aunt definitely knows what she's doing. She reminds me of my grandpa: tough as nails with a bleeding heart."

"I haven't met your grandfather. Does he live here?"

"He came to live with me two months ago. After my grandma died last spring, he didn't want to stay in Tulsa. I asked him to come live with me." His grandfather took him in when he'd run away from his abusive father. "When I was a teenager, he gave me a home and raised me. I figured I owed him. He loves my small ranch. Since he came, he's been increasing the number of abandoned animals at the ranch and raising them. Often, he finds them discarded along the highway, or sometimes they're left at our gate."

"I can't imagine abandoning an animal." Sarah took down two mugs. "How do you take your coffee?"

"Black."

She filled the cup and slid it toward Nick. "Anna loves animals. I need to get a dog for her. Our last one died six months ago, but with all that's been going on with the bombings and more people I'm trying to help, I've put that on the backburner."

"You're gonna get me a dog?" Anna asked from the entrance into the kitchen with Candy right behind her. "When?" Anna smiled from ear to ear, glancing back at her friend.

Sarah poured coffee into her mug. "Yes, when things settle down. Candy, would you like having a dog?"

The little girl nodded, moving into the kitchen and standing next to Anna.

"Good. You'll have a say in what dog we'll get."

Candy's eyes grew round. "I will?"

"Of course. You're part of this family now. Your mother asked me to take care of you if something happened to her. I was thrilled to say yes to her."

"You are? I can stay here?"

"Yes. You all take a seat, and I'll cut a couple of apples into slices for a snack. That should hold you both over until dinner." Sarah picked two big red apples from the refrigerator, withdrew a knife from a utensil drawer, and began to slice into an apple.

A loud gasp caused Sarah to swivel around.

Candy fled the room.

Nick plucked the knife from Sarah's hand. "I'll finish this. You take care of Candy."

"Thank you. I wasn't thinking. Anna stay here."

Sarah left the kitchen.

Nick wanted to wipe the pained look from her face. Sarah, as well as Candy, had a lot to deal with in a short time.

* * *

Sarah found Candy in Anna's bedroom, huddled between the bed and wall and clinging to her large Teddy bear. Sarah knelt down in front of the young girl. "I was focused on getting you and Anna a snack. I wasn't thinking, Candy."

She should have hidden her actions, but the child's reaction made Sarah wonder even more. Did Candy see something having to do with a knife? Did she witness her mother being stabbed? Seeing a possible weapon understandably was a trigger, and it might be for a long time. She hoped to get help for Candy. Sarah was too emotionally involved to counsel the girl formally. Besides, Sarah knew an excellent child psychologist. She planned to fulfill her role as the little girl's guardian and surrogate mother as Mary wanted.

Sarah placed her hand on Candy's back, hoping she would lift her head and make eye contact. For a long moment, the child remained frozen, curled into a ball. Then slowly she straightened and looked at Sarah. She opened her arms and drew Candy into her embrace. "I'll be here for you. I'm a good listener. It's good to talk about what's bothering you with another person. Keeping it bottled up inside is hard on you."

Candy clutched Molly against her side while sliding her arm around Sarah then pressing herself against her. Sarah's throat closed, emotions jamming her throat. She wanted to say something comforting, but the words refused to come out. All she could do was hold Candy as she cried against Sarah's chest. It broke her heart to listen to the anguish, but it was good for the child to release it. It was a small step toward healing.

As the sobs subsided, Candy leaned back, her eyes red, her cheeks tear stained. "I'm hungry."

Sarah chuckled, not surprised since Candy hadn't eaten anything that Sarah knew of today. "I'm glad. I've got apple slices for you and caramel to dip them into. I understand from Anna you love caramel more than chocolate. Let me tell you a secret. So do I."

"You do? Anna loves chocolate." Candy glanced at her Teddy bear. "But Molly loves caramel like me."

Sarah rose and held her hand out for the little girl. She decided eating in the kitchen might not be the best place for Candy right now. That too could trigger the child, especially if she'd seen what had happened in the kitchen earlier that day at her home. "Tell you what. Why don't we eat outside on the patio? It's a beautiful day. I'll have Anna and Nick bring the food out along with the lemonade in the refrigerator."

After Candy grabbed Sarah's hand and stood, they moved into the hallway. Candy released her grip and hugged Molly against her chest.

At the french doors in the den, Sarah paused. "I'll go tell Anna and Nick where we'll be. I'll be right back. Wait here." Sarah hurried into the kitchen and grabbed the pitcher of lemonade. "We're going to have a picnic out in the backyard. Bring the glasses, plates, apple slices, and caramel." She started for the doorway, stopped, and added, "Oh, and a wet cloth for the sticky fingers."

She headed back to the french doors, intending to make Candy's life as normal as possible. Nick and Anna joined them as they sat at the patio table. Everyone dug in, relishing the apple slices and caramel combination while downing lemonade in between bites, a contrast between sweet and sour. When Aunt Louise returned from the grocery store and announced she needed help putting up the food she bought, Anna and Candy volunteered to bring in the sacks. They hopped up. Before Sarah could stop both girls or at least give Candy the option to stay outside with her, they were racing toward the house and disappeared inside. It didn't seem the kitchen was a trigger, but the knife was. She prayed for the child's sake that she hadn't seen the actual murder.

"Did Candy say anything while you were talking with her?"

"I think she saw the man with a knife, possibly even attacking her mother, but not in their kitchen. Maybe while Mary was fleeing the guy in the living room. Although when I asked her, she wouldn't say anything. That can happen when a person has gone through a trauma. She's blocking it. I know a child psychologist who's very good at helping children. I've scheduled an appointment for tomorrow at eleven. She's working Candy in during her lunchtime." Tension wrapped its tight arms around her. Sarah released a long sigh while massaging the back of her neck. "I'm too emotionally involved to be the right person to work with Mary's daughter. I don't know if I could be objective. She needs someone who will comfort her, be there for her, and hold her when she needs it. As her guardian, I'll be that to her, not her therapist."

At the table sitting next to her, Nick swiveled his chair toward her at the same time she turned toward him. His knees bumped against hers, sending her chair back toward the table.

She chuckled. "As a kid, I used to spin around and around in a chair like this. I'd get dizzy. It was fun." That brief second of humor eased the stress. She needed that in order to be there for her two girls.

"I did that too as a kid."

"I want that in Candy's life. A child should never live in fear of her father—or for that matter, anyone. In her six years, she's gone through a lot. As I mentioned before, I've been talking with Anna about getting a dog. Now I need one more than ever. Candy needs a pet to love. I know that Mary was looking into getting one for her. I want to fulfill what Mary was planning."

"I might be able to help you. I have a litter of puppies at my ranch. They're eight weeks old. If you're up to it, maybe each girl can have a puppy."

"What kind of dog?"

"A mutt possibly part beagle and a sheepdog. The mother left her babies a couple of weeks ago. My pet, Bella, has taken over looking out for the puppies. I think they'll be medium-sized dogs."

She smiled. "Good. I'm not ready to have a large dog."

"Why don't you bring the girls to my ranch this weekend after church? Let them play with the puppies."

"That would be great."

"I'll let you know when. This case will take my focus until I find the murderer, but I'll need a little time off." He rose. "Which means I need to leave and follow up on a few leads."

"What leads?"

"Mainly Candy's father. Also, a couple on the block behind where Mary lived saw an old black pickup speed down the street around the time of the murder. Because the speed limit is twenty-five miles per hour, the man tried to get the license plate to report to the police. He only got the first three numbers."

"That's the only lead?"

"The few outside security cameras were taken out right before the murder, probably sometime during the night. The neighbor on the left said she saw a man jump over Mary's back fence around the time of the homicide."

"Could she describe the man?"

"All she saw from the back was a large man with medium length brown hair in jeans and a white T-shirt. The people who live in the house behind Mary don't have any outside cameras. They're in Dallas over the fall break. I talked to Mr. Holt on the phone. They left yesterday, and no one on either side of the Holts saw anything. We've asked the public for help and have a hotline they can call. And we're going through CCTV footage around that time although most of that is blocks away from Mary's street. We're also going through videotapes from security cameras on the surrounding streets."

"How do you do your job?"

"One day at a time. It can have its challenges but also rewards. Every time I solve a case and put a criminal in prison, I thank God for making the community a little safer. Someone has to stand up for the underdog. I'm determined to find Mary's killer."

"Now that Aunt Louise is back, I need to go to the office. I want to bring home Mary's file and see what I can find that might help you." She pushed to her feet and walked beside Nick toward the house. "I'll let you know right away if I find anything."

"I appreciate it. To be official, I'll be asking the court for a warrant for her records, but I would like your opinion on your notes."

"I want her killer found. Candy might never be safe until then. She'll need closure on her mother's death. If Mary's murder isn't solved, there will be an empty hole in her heart that will be hard to fill."

He opened the door and waited until she entered her house before following her inside. She continued to the front entrance. In the foyer, Nick turned toward her. With him inches away from her, she started to step back but didn't. His nearness gave her a sense of hope. Nick was a good detective, and she couldn't think of a better police officer to be the lead on Mary's case.

"Call me anytime you need me, or if you remember something that might help me figure out who killed Mary."

"I will."

His whole face transformed with a smile, his gaze intense as he looked at her as though there was a connection between them and they had known each other for many years. The times she'd talked to him, she'd always felt at ease with Nick, but she'd only moved here four years ago after her husband died.

"Bye, Sarah."

She shut the front door and hurried to the kitchen to check on Anna and Candy before she left. "I need to go to my office, but I won't be long. I've got good news. We're going to Nick's ranch to see some puppies this Sunday after church. He said you each can have a puppy. But if either one of you don't want to, that's fine. too." As she spoke two huge grins slowly filled Anna's and Candy's faces.

"No, Mom. We both want one."

Sarah gathered her purse and car keys then hugged each girl before leaving. She didn't want to be gone long. Besides bringing home her notes on Mary, she would get the list of her clients who had an appointment tomorrow and would personally call them when she returned home. She needed to be there with Candy and Anna on Friday. Thankfully, she didn't have as many appointments scheduled because of the school's fall break. But she would have to move those to the end of next week.

A few minutes later, she pulled into her parking space not far from the side door into the building complex. Her office was right inside near the entrance. She went into her private office through the second door. Sucking in a sharp breath, she came to a halt a few steps inside. Like the bedrooms at Mary's house, her office had been ransacked, all her items tossed onto the floor. With her eyes glued to one of her open filing cabinet drawers, she stuck her hand into her pocket for her cell phone. As she fumbled for it, something struck the back of her head. Pain shot through her skull. Her legs gave out.

FOUR

The sound of a door nearby slamming shut invaded Sarah's mind. Loud drumbeats pounded against her skull, shoving her back toward the black void. But she needed to stay awake. Her eyelids fluttered open while she struggled to sit up. Nausea roiled in her stomach. The room spun before her, and she leaned back against a cabinet near the door she'd used. She fumbled for her cell phone in her pocket and gripped it. As she lifted it to view the screen, she had to close her eyes until the room stopped rotating. She brought her arm down.

Call Nick. Now.

Sweat rolled down her face. She dug deep inside and forced herself to look at the phone and place a call to him.

"Sarah, are you at your office or home?" Nick asked while she tried to form the words she needed to say to him.

"My office. It was…" she struggled to keep her eyes open, "…ransacked. Someone hit my head from…" Her voice faded into silence.

"I'm on my way. How's your head?"

"Hurting." She straightened, trying to fight the pain, but instead, the hammering intensified in her head. "An elephant is tap dancing…"

"Stay with me. Don't hang up. I'm not far away. I should be there in five minutes."

He must have turned on his siren because she heard it through her cell phone. Thankfully, it wasn't too loud. She pressed the speaker button and let her phone drop into her lap. She leaned back again, using the filing cabinet as a support and closed her eyes, the darkness invading every recess of her mind.

"Sarah? Are you there?"

* * *

Nick pressed his foot down on the accelerator. Sarah still hadn't answered.

Alarm rose as the silence lengthened. "Sarah?"

He contacted the police dispatcher. He explained what was going down and requested an ambulance and a backup female officer to the crime scene. Two minutes later, his car screeched to a halt near the side door where her car was parked. He exited his SUV and raced for her office. As he headed for her private door, he noticed it was slightly opened. He withdrew his gun and treated the situation as though an intruder was inside. He didn't know what he was going into.

With his foot, he nudged the door open and planted himself in the entrance, his gun up and ready to use if needed. He moved a few steps inside and quickly scanned the large room. Sarah's desk and bookcases had been wiped clean, every item on them was on the floor now. Spying Sarah to the left propped up against a file cabinet, her eyes closed, he quickly covered the distance between them and knelt next to her. Her eyelids lifted halfway open while she moaned, her head sliding to the right. That was when he saw a stain of blood on the piece of furniture.

"Sarah?" He carefully cupped her face as

he moved her head, so he could see the severity of her wound. "Did you pass out?" he asked as he heard the side door to the building opening.

"I think so." She dragged those three words out.

"How long?"

Her face scrunched up as she tried to sit straighter. "Don't know." Her eyes, filled with pain and fear, connected with his. "A few minutes?"

Two EMTs came into the room with their gurney, followed by a police officer.

"I'll be here for you." Nick rose and stepped back to let the paramedics check out Sarah.

While they did, Nick approached Officer Maggie Landon and moved into the hallway. "I haven't had a chance to look around. I just got here a few minutes ago. I want to make sure Dr. Collins is all right. She has a nasty wound on the back of her head. This may have a connection to the murder of Mary Phillips. Sarah has the victim's child at her house. I need you to go there to keep an eye on Candy, but I don't want to scare the little girl."

"I can go home and change into regular clothes. I don't live far from Sarah."

"Good. I'll let her aunt know why you're showing up. In fact, Louise will probably want to go to the hospital."

"I'll take care of everything. Let Sarah know her family will be fine." Maggie headed for the exit.

"Call me if anything looks suspicious." Nick walked back into the office and looked at Sarah lying on the gurney. His attention riveted on her pale face. Pain gripped her, and he wanted to relieve it. He couldn't do anything about the physical pain, but he could ease her worry about her family. He came to her side. "Officer Landon is going to your house. I'll call your aunt and let her know what's going on."

She tried to smile, but the effort failed. "Thanks."

"Where are your keys to the office?"

"In my purse. It must be on the floor." She turned her head, lifting her index finger to point to her handbag.

Nick picked it up and brought it to her. "You'll need your medical information. I'd like to lock up your office after I process it."

"I need my locks changed." She could barely keep her eyes open.

"I'll take care of that. Don't worry." Nick squeezed her hand. "Your family will be all right."

This time her smile held for a couple of seconds before she closed her eyes.

The paramedics rolled the gurney out into the hallway. Nick locked the door, followed them from the building, and waited until they drove off before he went back inside.

When he reentered the office, he began his sweep of the room, assessing the damage. He started taking photos and trying to figure out what might be missing from the premises. He paused next to her desk, all the items on it scattered across the carpet, except her computer. It was gone. He rechecked everything in case he had missed it. Nothing.

If the intruder had only wanted the computer, then why the disarray? He might have been looking for something else too. Probably some items only Sarah could discern, especially with the file cabinet drawers left open and a couple of the files scattered on the floor as though the assailant had tossed them over his shoulder with the contents inside floating to the carpet. Nick called in for a crime scene tech to take fingerprints while he went to the hardware store and bought two good locks then arranged for a friend to install them. He needed to get to the hospital.

* * *

After Sarah was brought to a hospital room to stay overnight for observation, she scanned the area and asked the orderly to pull down the shade over the window. Tomorrow morning bright sunshine would flood the room and even the overhead light bothered her now. Her head pounded in spite of the medication the doctor gave her.

As the young man started for the door, she asked, "Is there any way to dim the lights?"

"Yes." He did what she'd requested then left.

With seven stitches in the back of her head, she gingerly laid it against the pillow, turning to the right side. The sound of the door opening drew her attention. When she spied Nick Davidson in the entrance, she slowly sat forward. "Thank you for sending Maggie to my house. She's staying the night, and that makes me feel a lot better. That and knowing Aunt Louise can take care of herself. Her training in the Marines taught her how to protect herself and others."

"I didn't realize she'd been a Marine. My grandfather and dad were too. There was a time I thought of joining up, but I ended up following in my uncle's footsteps. As a child, I'd always wanted to be a cop." Nick sat in the chair near the bed. "If you feel up to it, tell me what happened when you went to the office."

"I always come in by the side door." She adjusted her body, wincing while making the move. "Honestly, all I remember after that is unlocking my office and stepping inside. From my injury, I surmise I was hit from behind." Fighting to stay alert, she lifted her hand and rubbed her fingers across her forehead as though that would erase the thumping against her skull. The pain was better than an hour ago but only subdued. She could ask for more medication, but she didn't like taking pills. In her profession, she'd dealt with too many people who were addicted to pain meds.

"I'm going to put a guard at your door. I'd like to take you home tomorrow after the doctor gives you the okay. I want to take you to your office too."

"I hope that I'll remember more tomorrow?"

"I'll let your aunt know what I'm going to do."

"I appreciate that." She'd been battling to keep her eyes open, but slowly her eyelids drooped.

"I'm leaving. You need to get rest. I'll see you tomorrow."

Thinking about tomorrow reminded Sarah that she had to cancel Candy's appointment with the child psychologist at eleven or have Aunt Louise take her. The doctor wouldn't be releasing her until late morning or early afternoon. She hoped that Emma would move the appointment to later on Friday or better yet to Saturday. "Please keep Candy safe," she murmured to Nick as the darkness swamped her.

* * *

Keep Candy safe. All night long those words haunted Nick. He had to protect not just Candy but Sarah and Anna. Right now, standing in the middle of Sarah's office with her, he prayed she could help him find a clue that pointed to someone as she walked around and assessed the disarray. Was the disruption here connected to the death of Mary Phillips?

Lines of confusion deepened on her face, her eyebrows slashing downward toward each other. "The only thing missing is my laptop."

"How about your folders in the file cabinets?

"I scanned each one. I think they're completely there, but I'll need more time to make sure. I'll take Mary's file home with me and begin reading through the notes."

"Your doctor wants you to rest for a couple of days. Don't forget you have a nasty head wound."

She frowned. "I know. My head keeps telling me that. But I think I can go through Mary's file at least. I need a computer, so I can download my files from the cloud. I don't think whoever took my laptop can get into it, but if he did, he could erase everything I have stored in the cloud. That's many years of work gone in a click."

"I'll help in any way I can, even to tell you to rest when you need it."

Sarah tried to hide a yawn behind her hand.

"Let's go and buy that computer, then you need to go home and rest."

"There's that word again." Sarah moved toward the exit with a handful of files while Nick followed, carrying the rest of the ones she selected to take home.

After Nick settled behind the steering wheel, he backed out of the parking space and drove toward downtown. "The crime scene techs found a lot of fingerprints in your office. They're running them through the database, but there may be some that aren't in it. I'll show you the list we have when it's completed. If you know of someone who was in the room, but not on the list, I hope you'll be able to convince them to give us permission to take their prints."

"It'll be their choice. Besides, I don't see this being one of my patients. Mary's ex-husband is more likely her killer, not someone I'm counseling."

"I agree. Mary's ex is missing. The Texas and Oklahoma law enforcement agencies are looking for him."

"When did he go missing?"

Nick parked near a store that sold computers. "Four days before Mary was murdered. He'd been at work, complained he was sick, and left a few hours early. That's the last time anyone saw him. It's like he vanished into thin air."

"Do you think he's going to come after Candy?"

"Whoever killed Mary went through her

and Candy's bedrooms. If he is the killer, it's a good possibility he was looking for his daughter."

"But from what Mary told me about Jack Coleman, he didn't care about Candy. He didn't want children. So why would he come after her? It's too late to use taking Candy against Mary."

Nick shoved open the driver's side door. "He might not want her. He might want to kill her too." He glanced at Sarah.

A stunned look captured her face from her wide eyes to her mouth dropping open. "She isn't safe?"

"No. That's why I have a police officer at your house. Also, I've put out Coleman's photo, especially here in Cimarron City, as a person of interest in Mary's murder."

Sarah exited the car and leaned against it to keep herself upright while gripping the back of her neck.

Nick hurried around the hood and grasped her hand, his arms encircling her. "You all will be okay. I'll do everything I can to keep you and everyone else in your house safe."

"If it was Jack Coleman at my office yesterday, how did her ex-husband find out about me?" Sarah leaned slightly back and stared into his eyes.

"He could have been here for a while, probably casing her." He felt her shiver as it snaked down her.

"I need to get home. Let's go in and get the laptop."

Sarah looked exhausted in the short time she'd left the hospital. He was worried she was pushing herself too much. "Are you sure you can do it now?"

"Yes. I promise I'll rest when I get home. I can't lose my patient records and notes. Not everything is in the written files in my office, but it's on my computer."

Nick walked close to Sarah as they entered the store and slowly headed to the left toward the computer section. She knew what she wanted and bought it quickly. Again, he escorted her from the place, keeping her close in case she lost her balance or footing. When she slipped into the passenger seat and looked up at him, exhaustion lined her face even more. She collapsed back, her eyes closing as she gingerly laid her head against the seat.

"Sarah, are you all right?"

"Just a little tired."

"You'll be home soon." Nick closed her door and hurried to the other side.

As he drove to her house, he slid his gaze to Sarah, checking on her. She drew in deep breaths, and a hint of color had returned to her cheeks. "When you arrive home, you should lay down."

She smiled for a couple of seconds. "You don't know how hard that can be when you have a child, and now with Candy it will be even harder."

"I plan to stay and relieve Officer Landon."

"Thanks. With what's been happening, that makes me feel safer."

He turned into her driveway and parked his SUV. Officer Landon had left her patrol car on the street in front of Sarah's house. The front door flew open, and both Anna and Candy ran outside, making a beeline for Sarah as she stood and held onto the front seat passenger's door.

"We missed ya," Anna said while both girls put their arms around her.

"I'm glad to be here too." She hugged them. "Let's go inside." After passing the sack with the computer in it to him, she clasped hands with Anna and Candy, allowing them to guide her toward the house.

Nick followed, his gaze assessing the

area. He was the last to go inside and paused at the entrance, taking one last appraisal before closing the door. He turned and nearly ran into Sarah. She stood in the foyer staring at a vase full of blue carnations.

FIVE

"Girls, go see if Aunt Louise can fix me a cup of tea." The second Anna and Candy left the entry hall, Sarah wilted back against Nick, energy draining from her legs.

He clasped her arms and held her in front of him. "What's wrong?"

"This is the third bouquet of flowers I've received like these in the past couple of weeks." She waved her hand toward the vase. "There's never a note left with the carnations."

"Delivered to your house each time?"

"No, only to my office. This is the first one sent here, which means the person might have known about what happened at my office yesterday afternoon. Was it reported on the news?"

"No. I kept it quiet. I didn't want a circus outside your house."

She turned to look at him. "Good. It would be hard to explain to the girls."

"Who canceled today's appointments for you?"

"My secretary, Allie Johnson. So, it could have been one of them, although Allie only told them an emergency had come up."

"It could have been someone watching what's going on with you."

"A stalker?"

"It's possible." What color that had returned to her cheeks disappeared.

Aunt Louise came into the foyer. She carried a cup of tea. Following her, Anna carried a basket of goodies while Candy had two plates and napkins.

"I thought you might be hungry too," Aunt Louise said.

"Mmm. These muffins smell wonderful." Sarah took the mug from her aunt. "Let's go into the den."

"Nick, what would you like to drink?" Aunt Louise asked as she started for the kitchen.

"Coffee, if you have it."

"I do. That's my favorite drink. Be right back. Girls, you need to get the lemonade I made for you."

While Anna and Candy went with her aunt, Sarah moved toward the den at the back of the house. "I don't want the girls to know anything about what happened to me or about the vases of carnations. Especially Candy. She needs to be shielded. I want to make her life as normal as possible while being here for her." Sarah sat on the brown leather couch and put her mug on a coaster on the coffee table. "I wish that we didn't need to have an officer here. I appreciate she's in plain clothes, but her patrol car is out in front of the house. When I talked with Aunt Louise earlier this morning, she mentioned the girls were in the living room looking out the window last night at the patrol car. Maggie walked around outside a lot, but when she came inside, Anna had tons of questions for her. She wanted to go outside and see the police car better. Candy began crying and ran upstairs to her bedroom."

Nick checked to see if anyone was coming into the den. Then he turned his attention to her. "Having the patrol car outside the house is one way to keep whoever came after Mary Phillips away from here. It's a good deterrent. When I'm not here, I want a patrol officer in place."

"I understand. I'll talk with Candy later. I need something to divert the girls' attention. Any suggestions?"

"As mentioned before, a dog could be effective. Rest today and tomorrow, then after church on Sunday, I can take you and the girls to the ranch to pick out their puppies. Whatever works for you."

"That's a good suggestion. I'll manage. I plan to take it really easy today and tomorrow. I should be able to go out for several hours by Sunday. Aunt Louise took Candy to see Dr. Emma Reichs for her eleven o'clock appointment today to become acquainted with Emma. I was hoping I could go for the first session, but as you know, my doctor at the hospital was running late. I'll be going with Candy when she sees the child psychologist Monday after school." She heard the girls and Aunt Louise coming into the room. She forced a smile and looked at them. "I was about to get up and see what was taking you all so long." Looking at Anna and Candy, she patted the couch on each side. "Come sit by me. I missed both of you."

"What happened?" Anna asked.

"I fell and hit my head, but I'm going to

be fine." She hated twisting what happened to her, but the girls didn't need to worry about what was going on. When she'd talked to Aunt Louise last night, she'd come up with the story about Sarah falling. She slipped her arms around each one and brought them up against her. "Did you all help Aunt Louise with lunch?"

"Yes," her daughter said while Candy nodded.

"I've got a surprise for both of you. On Sunday after church, we're going to Nick's ranch to look at his puppies. You both can pick one out to be yours if you want."

"We can?" Candy's eyes widened.

Anna clapped then pumped her arm in the air. "Yes! I've wanted a puppy forever." She stretched out the last word.

Candy sat forward and straightened her shoulders. "My very own dog?"

Sarah cupped the child's face and smiled. "Yes, your own puppy. But with you being the person in charge, you'll have to learn to take care of the dog—feed it, give it water, and love it. Are you ready for that?" She swung her attention from Candy to Anna. "That goes for both of you."

Candy nodded while Anna said, "Yes, we're ready."

Sarah hugged the girls, kissing the top of each child's head. Candy and Anna snuggled even closer to her. Even if Jack Coleman wasn't Mary's killer, Sarah would need to keep that man away from Candy. She needed a chance to live in a protected environment. As Sarah lifted her gaze, it connected with Nick's. In that moment, she felt as though she wasn't alone, that Nick was here to help her, even beyond his duties as a law enforcement officer. A calmness enveloped her, and she smiled at him.

Aunt Louise, who remained at the entrance into the den, finally said, "Girls, we need to let Sarah rest, and I want you both to help me clean up the mess from lunch. Then we'll need to make a list of stuff you'll need for your pets. We'll have to buy them before we bring the puppies home."

"Can we do the list first?" Anna asked.

"Okay. Go get paper and a pencil." Aunt Louise chuckled as the girls raced from the room. "I wish I had their energy."

Sarah looked at the entrance. "How did the flowers end up in the house?"

"When we came home from Candy's appointment, they were on the porch in front of the door. I thought they were from someone who knew you were in the hospital."

"Was Officer Landon with you all at the therapist?" Sarah asked.

"Yes. She drove us."

Nick frowned. "How long were you all gone?"

"About an hour and a half. I thought you would love them because they're carnations and you love the color blue. I figured they were from a friend." Her aunt's gaze flittered back and forth between Sarah and Nick. "What's going on?"

"That's a good question. The carnations today were my third bouquet in the past two weeks. No card. No idea who sent them." Sarah crossed her arms, a chill encasing her. "I don't have a good feeling about the flowers. Something sinister is behind them."

* * *

Sunday, Nick pulled up to the front of his house, glancing at Sarah in the seat beside him. After he convinced her to relax and let him be her chauffeur, he drove his car from the church's parking lot while Sarah left her car there to be picked up later. In the church's parking lot, her paleness had leaked through her facial features, and her brown eyes hadn't sparkled as usual. The past few days had taken a toll.

Nick looked over his shoulder at the girls in the backseat. Anna had a huge smile on her face while Candy kept her head down and her arms around her Teddy bear. "Are you two ready to see the puppies?"

Candy looked up. A resounding yes came from both girls.

Sarah drew his attention. The color in her cheeks had returned, but the worry in her eyes was still there. He hated seeing that look. He still had no idea who broke into her office and took her laptop. Thankfully, she was able to recover the files from her cloud account. But the question still unanswered was why the intruder took the laptop. What was he looking for on her computer? How was the break-in connected to the murder of Mary Phillips? If it was the killer, why did he risk being caught to get information on Mary? She was dead. Sarah couldn't find anything on her laptop that would indicate another person besides Mary's ex-husband as having a motive to murder her. Was the break-in somehow connected to another client Sarah was treating? A lot of files had been rifled through.

"Nick, are you coming?" Sarah's voice penetrated his thoughts and brought him back to the present.

He glanced at the backseat, empty, except for Candy's Teddy bear, then at Sarah opening her door. A few feet from his SUV Bella, his dog, sat between the little girls while they petted her. "Sure. Just thinking about what you told me this morning concerning the files on your computer."

She paused and twisted toward him. "I wish I had good news, but the files were intact after I went through the mess and straightened them up. Later today, you'll have a chance to read Mary's file. I'm sending it to the medical examiner, per his request and the court warrant."

"Anything else on your computer, besides her files, that might give us an idea who broke into your office."

"Not that I know of. Tomorrow when the girls are at school, I want to go back to my office and begin cleaning up now that you've released the crime scene."

"Then I'll come with you."

"Will Maggie be at my house when the girls come home from school? With all that's happened, I don't think Candy's safe there

73

without a police presence, especially when I'm not there to protect her."

"Either I'll be there, or Maggie will. She's the best choice since the girls know her. Candy isn't the only one who needs protection. You do too. You were assaulted. We have no idea why other than someone might want information on Mary. Why would they since she was already dead? If it was Coleman, why did he go to your office? What would be on your laptop that would help him? If he was the murderer, he knew where Mary lived. Instead of finding answers, I only have more questions." Nick looked past Sarah and smiled. "It looks like Bella has two new friends." He gestured toward the girls petting and hugging his mutt.

Sarah looked at Anna and Candy and grinned. "Bella is adorable."

"Yeah, she was exactly what I needed when she came to my ranch, so thin her ribs were showing. I immediately took her in and have never regretted that decision. Her presence helped me to work through nearly dying after being shot on duty. God sent Bella."

"When was that?"

"Five years ago." Nick hated remembering that evening when he'd gone to a house because of a domestic disturbance called in by a neighbor. "Bella was in bad shape, and so was I from being shot on duty. We helped each other." He opened his driver's side door and came around to hold his hand out to help Sarah. She stood inches from him, her scent of vanilla teasing his senses, bringing back memories of helping his mother bake sugar cookies and eating so many he got sick. But that never stopped him from eating more later. "Bella has a way of zeroing in on a person who needs her comfort." He pointed at his dog, a combination of a bull terrier and a corgi, lying on the ground face up while Candy stroked her stomach over and over, plastered against his pet's side.

"Bella's working her magic right now. I can see it on Candy's face."

"Let's go to the barn and see which puppy they want to choose." Nick gestured toward the building a couple of hundred yards away and turned toward Sarah, his focus totally on her.

Sarah chuckled. "If they want to choose? Didn't you hear them on the way to your ranch? That's all they talked about. Candy's been quiet most of the time but not when she talked with Anna about the puppies."

Nick glanced over his shoulder at the black barn. Candy and Anna both tackled pulling the large, heavy door open. "They're fast. I keep the doors closed when no one's in the barn so that some of the animals don't wander off. They've been known to do that." He took Sarah's hand and hurried toward the black building.

Before he could call out to the girls to wait, Sarah said, "Stop. We don't want any of the animals to get loose."

Candy froze while Anna tried to poke her head through the small opening.

Nick rushed forward and gripped the door. "I like to give the puppies room to move around but remain safe. We've had a coyote nearby the past few weeks. I think it's moved on, but I don't want to take a chance with any animal not able to protect itself."

Sarah leaned toward him and whispered, "Bella protects herself?"

"Yes." Nick swung the door wide, and the girls darted inside and ran toward the puppies. "Bella was about two or three when she came to me. She knew how to take care of herself. She's very protective of me, but her love has helped me through stressful situations, especially that time I was shot on the job. Plus, she's a great watchdog. The coyote left the area because he couldn't get past Bella."

While Candy and Anna went from one puppy to the next, Sarah scanned the barn. "Where's the puppies' mother?"

"She left a couple of weeks ago. Bella's been looking out for them since their mama left."

"Because of the coyote?"

"No. The puppies' stray mama could take care of herself. She can handle a coyote. The puppies were eating solid food by the time she left, and I guess she thought I would take care of her five babies."

"Can I have two, Mom?" Anna held one in each hand.

"No. One for each of you. Taking care of one is a lot of work, and I know you both want to do your best."

Candy cuddled the smallest puppy against her. "I want this one. She needs me."

"And I'm picking Charlie." Anna put down a squirmy pup and lifted up the other one.

"You're calling this one Charlie?" Nick asked as the puppy not chosen raced away.

"Yeah, after my daddy."

Nick glanced at Candy. "What's your puppy's name?"

The child's eyebrows slashed downward as she focused totally on the animal. "I don't have one—yet."

Sarah smiled. "I had a dog when I was growing up, and it took me days to come up with the name. The perfect one will come to you."

"Now that you have your pets, let's go up to the house. My grandpa has lunch prepared. He'll want to see which puppies you picked out, so bring them with you." After the two girls and Sarah left, Nick closed the barn door and started for the one-story ranch house with Bella at his side.

"Are we going to eat outside?" Sarah asked as she walked next to Nick.

"Yes. Today's too pretty to stay inside."

"Good. I hate that Anna and Candy have to stay inside so much at my house. Tomorrow, they'll be going back to school. Candy's in the same classroom as Anna. Their teacher goes to our church. I've talked to Whitney Sherman about what's happened to Candy and how she's coping with her mother's death."

"How's she coping?"

"She's holding it in. I find her talking to

Molly, her Teddy bear, but she hasn't said much to me since that first day. I'm going to work half days this week. My secretary's been straightening my office after the police released it. After I take the girls to school, I'll finish it. There are some areas Allie thought I should take care of. Mostly the hard copy of my files that I didn't bring home from my office on Friday. Later, on Monday, I'll be going with Candy to her appointment with the child psychologist."

The front door to his house swung open, and his grandpa stood in the entrance. "It's about time y'all came. I was about to eat all the food I made for lunch." He looked from Candy to Anna. "I hope you two are hungry. The grill's ready to go for our hamburgers and hot dogs. But the best food today is my ultimate brownies, a secret recipe that's been in my family for years. Ready?"

Anna nodded while Candy brought her puppy up against her cheek.

"Then let's go." Grandpa held the screen door open while the two girls headed into the entry hall. Nick followed them. Sarah's cell phone rang, and he looked over his shoulder at her as she talked to whoever was on the other end. As she listened to her caller, Sarah's eyes grew as round as a basketball.

Nick signaled his grandpa to take the little girls out back. "Bella, go with Bernie." He pointed to the trio leaving the foyer. Then he turned toward Sarah.

Something was wrong. She disconnected the call.

"What happened?"

"Aunt Louise came home from church to find my house vandalized. Every room trashed."

SIX

Sarah picked her way through the rubbish littering her living room floor. "In less than a week, I've stood in the middle of a trashed room three times. What's going on? The destruction seems so familiar, as though the same person tossed Mary's house, my office, and now my home. Is he looking for a specific object or trying to freak me out? Is Candy somehow tied to all three break-ins, or are two different agendas playing out here?"

"I don't have the answer right now." Nick crossed the room and stopped a couple of feet in front of her. "Like your office, you'll need to go through your house and let us know if anything's missing. Can your aunt assist you? What's missing will help us come up with some answers, hopefully."

His nearness sent her heart rate soaring. "She's already going through the kitchen. That's her domain, and she knows more of what's in there than I do. She's been a lifesaver for me. What did your grandfather say the girls were doing? Are they okay?"

"They're fine. He's been helping them with the two puppies, showing them how they can take care of their pets. You don't need to worry about them. My grandfather is great with kids and capable of protecting them."

"With everything happening so quickly, all I want is to make sure they're all right, especially Candy with all that's been going on." Tears of anger and frustration filled her eyes. She saw Nick through a watery haze, the lines of concern on his face.

"I won't stop until I find who's doing this. He's not going to get away with this." He moved closer to her. "You need a better security alarm system. Somehow, he got into this house without the alarm going off. You have one laser in the foyer that points down the hallway to the two downstairs bedrooms and bathroom. He could slip by the beam and go up the stairs, and if he crawled along the hallway low like a pet, he could go into the rooms on the first floor, which he obviously did, based on the destruction in there. Your windows aren't wired. It looks like he left out your bedroom window. It's shut but unlocked."

"Could he have come in through that window?" Sarah asked as Aunt Louise entered the living room and paused by the couch. She saw distress in Aunt Louise's eyes for the first time ever. Knowing her aunt's background and her capability to take care of herself produced a heightened fear in Sarah.

"No, unless you keep that window unlocked all the time. The footprints under the sill indicate someone was there recently and only indicated he left by that way, one set only going away from the house. Last night's rain softened the soil. The same boots left a deep impression in the backyard flower bed, so I believe he departed the yard that way."

"I have never left any windows unlocked. Not even the ones upstairs." Folding her arms across her chest, Sarah shivered. "Especially considering I had a peeping Tom a month ago."

"Did you report it to the police?"

She shook her head. "I was really tired

and wasn't sure at all. I haven't noticed anything since then."

Nick frowned. "Next time you call me if you notice something odd. I'd feel better coming out here and making sure it wasn't a peeping Tom."

Aunt Louise stepped over a drawer and its content and covered the distance between her and them. "I think I know how he could have gotten inside if the doors and windows were locked."

Sarah thought about how hectic this morning had been before they went to church. She took the girls in her car with Officer Landon following them while Aunt Louise had a few things to do before she left in her car. "How did the person get inside?"

Aunt Louise released a long breath. "I was taking some dishes to the car for the brunch between services. I forgot something in my bedroom and ran back into the house to get it. I don't think I locked the kitchen door to the garage when I came back outside. I was running late."

"When I left, I put the garage door down," Sarah said. "As I drove away, I saw it in the rearview mirror going down, so if that was the way the intruder got inside, that means he was in the garage. The question is when did he get inside there." The thought sent her pulse racing through her veins.

"It was down when I returned to the garage."

Sarah frowned. Had there been enough time for someone to slip into the garage and go into the house? Sarah could picture the intruder hiding behind the large garbage can on the side of the house for an opportunity to get into the garage and then into her home undetected. There were several places someone could hide near the door into her kitchen, especially when they were rushing around to get to church on time. They might never know how it happened. "How long were you gone from the garage?"

"No more than three or four minutes."

"Why would someone take that kind of risk? For Candy? Or something else? The person had to be outside waiting for us to leave."

"It's common knowledge that we go to church on Sunday." Aunt Louise began to pick up some items on the floor. "What if the break-in at your office and house doesn't have anything to do with Mary and Candy? Someone is leaving you bouquet of flowers, and you had a possible peeping Tom."

"Where did you receive the flowers?" Nick raked his hand through his dark brown hair.

"At the office. Only once at home."

"You have a stalker." Nick's scowl and comment dominated Sarah's full attention.

"At first, I thought it was a client who was giving me the bouquets as a thank you. I have patients who won't say it to me but have left little gifts."

"The same gift over and over?"

"For instance, Mary loved to bake and would bring me some of what she had made."

"But she didn't hide her identity when she did that." Aunt Louise finger-combed her bangs off her forehead.

"Some of the people I work with are emotionally fragile. I can't have the police questioning them when nothing bad has happened." Sarah held up her hand to stop Nick from saying anything. "I realize the behavior, especially in the last week, is escalating, and it could become a problem. I got sidetracked with Mary's murder. I don't know what to do. I have to consider not only Anna but Candy now. What do you suggest, Nick?"

"Pack up and come to my ranch to stay until the trouble is over."

* * *

Later Sunday night, Nick came into his house after walking around outside to check for anything that didn't belong. He, his grandpa, and Louise intended to take turns at night keeping watch. Earlier, he had to talk his grandfather out of guarding them from ten in the evening to seven in the morning. That was too long, especially for a man who had recently turned seventy. Louise overheard him and his granddad arguing on the front porch and came outside to settle it. Nick smiled at the take-charge woman who declared she would do her part too. They both agreed with Nick that Sarah had enough to do to recover and help Candy deal with her loss. And besides, Louise pointed out that she and Grandpa could rest after the two girls left for school.

Nick stood on the back patio with Bella sitting next to him. The sun was vanishing as it sank below the tree line. Bella growled low. She jumped up. Was someone watching the house from the woods about two hundred yards away? At first, he thought of leaving to investigate the rear part of his ranch where the vegetation was thicker than the rest of his land. The darkness would hinder him, but tomorrow morning before he went to work, he would take Bella and have a look around the area.

The sound of the door opening behind him didn't distract him from watching the tree line. Bella would have alerted him if it was someone who didn't belong. Two puppies ran toward Bella followed by Anna and Candy. His dog took charge of the pups and guided them to the grass, making sure they stayed close to the patio while they played and went to the bathroom.

Sarah stepped up to his right side. "The sunset is beautiful. You have a great view."

"Yes." But his attention wasn't focused on the red, orange, and yellow streaks blending into each other. He stared at the woods. "Did the girls feed their pets?"

"Yes, and they gave the puppies water although a lot of it sloshed onto the tile floor. I suggested next time they should fill a glass and pour it into their bowls."

"I imagine all four of them will go to bed early tonight."

"I agree. They haven't stopped since the girls woke up early this morning. I saw how tired Bernie was when we finally returned from my house. I'm glad he got in a nap before dinner."

Nick chuckled. "He's the one who keeps telling me I need to get married and have children. I wonder after a few days with the girls here if he'll still think that's a good idea."

"After the stories he told about his two daughters and three sons, he probably will. I heard how important family is to him. I think it is too. I love mine and always wanted more children after Anna was born, but my husband was killed by a drunk driver."

Nick turned toward her, staring at the beauty he saw in Sarah that had nothing to do with her pleasing features. "Is that why you agreed to be Candy's guardian if anything happened to Mary?"

She nodded, their gazes bound together for a long moment.

Until the air filled with Bella barking.

Nick swiveled around toward the grove behind his house. Bella raced toward the trees.

He should have listened to his gut feeling. "Get them inside and lock the door," he whispered to Sarah then jogged toward his dog.

He glanced back to make sure the girls and Sarah were inside. When she shut the door, he returned his full attention to the woods and withdrew a small but bright flashlight that he had in his jacket pocket in case he needed it. He reached around and gripped his Glock beneath his light jacket in a holster against his waist at his back, not the most ideal place to hide it, but he had to conceal it for the kids' sake.

At his side, Bella continued to growl. He'd trained her to find and go after animals like coyotes and foxes that went after the pets he had on the ranch. "Search."

Bella shot forward and disappeared into the woods. Nick sprinted after his dog into the darker terrain under the trees. He clicked on his flashlight and swept the area before him. Barking, Bella made a beeline for a coyote. It raced away from her. She followed several yards until Nick said, "Heel."

His pet came to a stop, whirled around, and returned to his side. "Good, Bella."

Before going back to his house, he switched off his flashlight and waited for his eyes to adjust to the darkness creeping through the trees. Nothing.

He allowed himself to relax for a few seconds before he swiveled toward the house and headed back. When he came through the entrance into his home, Sarah stood nearby, gripping the back of a lounge chair. The concern on her face and her narrowed brown eyes as she assessed he was unharmed touched him. Relief washed away the tension in her stance, and she relaxed against the chair back.

"Why did Bella bark?" Sarah asked as her fingers dug into the fabric on the lounger.

"A coyote was intruding on her territory. Like I told you. She defends her home." For a few seconds all he wanted to do was hold Sarah, reassure her he would protect her. This time it was a coyote. Next time it might not be an animal but a man. He couldn't let down his guard.

"Oh, good." The stress that had crept back into her expression completely melted away.

"Where are the girls?"

"Taking their bath and getting dressed for bed. A lot has happened today, and they have to wake up early to go to school tomorrow."

"It's only seven thirty."

Sarah chuckled. "I didn't say they would be going to bed right away. I told them we could play a game if they got ready early. They don't think they're ready to go to sleep, but I know Anna. She won't last an hour. The same for Candy. She's having a hard time keeping her eyes open."

"She's dealt with a lot these past four days."

"Her fall break wasn't anything like what Mary had wanted for her. She'd planned to go to the Tulsa Zoo last Friday with Candy and Anna while I worked."

"Maybe you can go at Christmas. It's always decorated and festive. Hopefully by then, I'll have this all figured out and the perpetrator in jail."

"That's a good suggestion. Besides, Candy needs time to adjust to her new situation. Until things settle down, I don't see that happening. She has a birthday in a week. I want to plan something fun for her next weekend."

Nick smiled. "How about inviting her friends to the ranch? We have two horses. The kids can ride them. One is especially gentle and would be good for the child who doesn't know how to ride a horse. Also, maybe there would be someone who would want to adopt one of the remaining three puppies. My only concern would be that you know the parents of the children you invite."

"I do. I'll keep it confined to the girls and boys in Candy's and Anna's class."

"Good. I'll help any way I can when I have the time." Drawn to Sarah, Nick stepped closer to her. Her faint scent of vanilla wafted to him.

When he had invited her to stay at the ranch until the killer was found, he'd been surprised initially at what he'd done, but there was something that happened deep inside him when he saw her bleeding and dazed. He knew then he would do anything to keep her alive and unharmed. Which astonished him because after he'd been shot and nearly died, he'd been determined to keep himself emotionally uninvolved in his cases. He'd been too occupied in that case, which had put him in a situation he could have avoided if he hadn't rushed in without thinking first.

"Nick, are you okay? We don't have to have a party here. We could do something at the Pizza and Fun Palace."

"No, that would be too chaotic trying to keep track of the kids there. They would all want to go to different rides and games. We wouldn't have any control of who was there."

"Then why the frown?"

His smile returned. "Honestly?"

She nodded.

The urge to erase the concern in her expression swamped him. He lifted his hand and cupped her face for a few seconds before he dropped his arm and kept it at his side. "When I was shot five years ago and nearly died, I rushed into a warehouse because I was following the man who fled the scene of a domestic dispute that evolved into an assault and a murder. He left his wife beaten badly and a neighbor shot and killed for trying to help her. After help arrived, I went after the killer. He had set up an ambush, and I went headlong into it without backup. He'd carefully planned it. When it comes to domestic violence, I have a hard time being impartial."

"I know what you're going through. I had a problem like that too, ignoring what I should have done to keep myself safe when I faced a patient's spouse who had lost it in my office. I tried to talk him down instead of backing away. He was six feet, seven inches tall and muscular. I knew he had a hair-trigger temper." Sarah sighed. "When he barged into my office, I should have called the police immediately, but I let him vent. He left, but when I went to my car half an hour later, he was in the parking lot waiting for me. He waved a gun in my face, demanding that I stop talking to his wife. I prayed, and God answered. Two police officers showed up, and they managed to step in and get the weapon. I found out later that Allie called the police because of the shouting."

"When did this happen, and who was it? Do you work with the man's wife now? He could be the person sending you flowers."

She shook her head. "The man went to jail for three months, and when he was released, he left Cimarron City."

"Where did they go?"

"His wife left him, and he moved to Oregon where his family lived."

"I need his name to make sure he's still there."

"He's Harry Young, and he settled in Portland. This situation made me realize I shouldn't work with different members of a family, although technically, he wasn't my patient, just his wife. That's why I'm having someone else besides me to help Candy deal with her mother being killed. I'm afraid my emotions might get in the way. Besides, I don't work with young children. Although, I do help some teenage clients."

The issue of domestic abuse was important to both of them. Another reason he was attracted to Sarah. "I don't know how you do everything. Helping your patients. Being involved at church. Taking care of your daughter and now Candy." Again, he felt a pull toward Sarah. She was an amazing woman. But he had to keep his distance. There was no place for emotions in this case, yet he had invited Sarah and her family to stay at the ranch where he could protect her. He knew the landscape and area better than her home or somewhere new.

"There are times I don't know how I do everything." Sarah glanced toward the doorway then back at him. "If you're sure about having the party here, then I accept the opportunity," she whispered. "I need to go check on the girls."

"Before you leave, I want you to think about any of your patients who might be behind the flowers. Also, consider this may be someone who isn't one of your clients. Make a list of possible people who could do it. You don't have to tell me if anyone on it is your patient."

"So, is the killer responsible for the flowers or someone else?"

"I think the flower person is separate from the killer, but the trashed house and office could be connected to," Nick checked the entrance, "the person who murdered Mary and who injured you. That's the main reason for you all being here."

"What if it's both?"

"That would mean most likely it was Jack Coleman."

"If it's Mary's ex-husband, then he's after me because I was helping Mary and will have guardianship of Candy soon."

Nick withdrew a photo from his back pocket. "This is a current photo of Jack Coleman. Study it, and if you see anyone that looks like that, let me know right away. He's still the main person of interest in Mary's death."

"Mary got rid of all her pictures of him. This is the first time I've seen him." Sarah took the photo and studied it. Her forehead crinkled, and her eyes narrowed. "I've seen this man."

SEVEN

Wednesday afternoon, Sarah sat across from Joe Burns, her last patient of the day. "Can you change the results of what happened when that car slammed into yours?"

"No. He came out of the blue. I didn't see him coming." Joe hung his head and stared at his lap.

If anyone could understand what her patient was going through, it was her. Sarah hadn't been in the car when her husband died in a wreck caused by a drunk driver, but the what ifs still plagued her after it sank in that he was gone for good. Then she'd had a friend ask her, "If you could bring your husband back from the dead, would you?"

"No," she'd answered. "That's an impossibility."

"So, you recognize you can't alter the past. Why, then, are you dwelling on what can never change?"

Her friend had been correct. Going over and over about what happened in the past wouldn't change it. Worrying about the future and what might occur only stressed a person.

We don't know what's to come. Only the Lord. He wants us to focus on the present. For her, that had been a difficult lesson to learn.

"Joe, I've learned the hard way that as much as I wish I could revise what happened to my husband, who died in a car wreck he didn't cause, I can't change what happened. The past can't be rewritten, but when we dwell on it, we don't move on. I wish we were always in control, but we aren't. We get stuck in what already occurred—like quicksand that sucks us down into the mire. The more we fight the quicksand, the quicker we are swallowed up by it. Is that what you want for your life? Is that what Jane would want for you? Stuck in the bog, not able to move forward. You came to me because you have two children who are looking to you to help them through their grief of losing their mother."

He lifted his head. "I'm trying. I thought time would take care of it, but she died eighteen months ago, and I'm still consumed with thoughts of her."

"I've been where you are. There's nothing wrong with thinking about your wife. You miss her, and that's okay. She was the mother of your two children. I'm not telling you to go out and find another woman to love. I'm asking you to listen to your kids. They need you to help them grieve their mother's death. Helping them will help you get through the depression you're suffering. That's part of the stages of grief. Try to turn that grief into accepting what occurred eighteen months ago."

"But I'm alone."

"No, you aren't. You have two children who need to know how to deal with their feelings. By focusing on them, you aren't concentrating on something you can't change. What are you doing with your kids as a family?"

Joe stared at the wall to the left. "Schoolwork when they're having trouble. We go to church together. That was important to Jane."

"That's a start. Between now and our next appointment, I want you to plan and go on an outing as a family. It can be something as simple as going to the movie or to the park to play basketball. During that time, concentrate on your children and their needs. Then tell me how you feel about the experience."

"But what if I mess up?"

Sarah stood. "Remember the same can be said about our future. We don't know what will happen in the next hour. Worrying about the past or the future takes away our focus on the present. Don't worry about messing up." She smiled. "Believe me. I've done my share of messing up with my child. Live in the moment. It's less stressful. Don't take my word. The Lord feels that way."

Joe rose. "Thanks. You've given me something to think about."

She walked with him to the exit that led into the hallway. After her patient left, Sarah leaned back against the door, surveying her office that had finally been cleaned up and returned to its original state.

Exhaustion took a tight hold on her. She'd only worked half a day as a counselor, but she'd put in eight hours because she'd had to finish organizing her files that had been messed up. Still, she hadn't found anything missing in those files. The only thing that had been taken was her laptop. Why all the mess? What was the motive behind trashing the office? Was it her "admirer"? Or Mary's killer?

She pushed off the door, closed the distance to the desk, and grabbed her purse. As she withdrew her keys, she looked at the new ones. On Monday, Nick changed out her locks here and at her house. He'd also set up a few motion-sensitive surveillance cameras that weren't obvious on the outside of her house and here at the office. Because of the nature of her work and the laws that protected her clients, the cameras at the office were only turned on when she was there alone or after hours. If someone broke into her office again, the intruder wouldn't realize he was being filmed, especially since all the cameras had night-vision mode. Nick even installed one of the motion sensor cameras in the short hallway of her private entrance. It had to be the way the assailant got in because the main corridor had cameras, and no one showed up on it other than her secretary leaving for the day. Nick thought the guy who robbed her knew how to avoid any surveillance at Sarah's place of work, a professional office building, which indicated he possibly was one of her patients.

She needed to pick up Candy from her session with Dr. Emma Reichs because her aunt had to take Anna to her ballet class. Sarah was going to take Candy to the studio. She'd expressed an interest in doing the same as Anna. Keeping Candy active would help her and give her an outlet for her emotions.

As Sarah left out her side door, she only had to take a couple of steps to her car, but she stopped dead in her tracks, glaring at a picture carved into her driver's side door. She dug into her purse, pulled out her cell phone, and placed a call to Nick, the drawing taunting her. While she turned her back on her Chevy, the phone rang as she surveyed her surroundings. She couldn't shake the feeling of being watched.

* * *

Nick gripped his cell as he listened to what happened in the parking lot at Sarah's office. "I'm across town. I'll be there as soon as I can. Don't get into the car until I check it out. Go back inside until I arrive." At least now he could rule out Harry Young. The Portland police confirmed he was living there and hadn't left town.

"I've got to pick up Candy. I can't be late. It will stress her out. Allie is still here. I'll see if she can take me to Emma's clinic. Can you pick me up there?"

"Yes, I'll meet you there after I swing by where your car is. Did you park near the door into the building?"

"Yes, the second spot to the left."

He'd rather Sarah wait for him, but he understood why she didn't want to. It didn't take much for Candy to retreat into herself. Any loud sound spooked the child. Last night, his grandfather had dropped a pan in the kitchen. Candy scurried under the table, curled into a ball, and hid her face.

Nick pulled into the parking lot, exited his SUV, and strode to the space where Sarah's car was. He spied the etched picture of a woman being hung on her driver's side door. His stomach roiled at its sight. He ground his teeth, realizing the person taunting her was escalating. He stepped to the door and peered inside. A red carnation lay on the front seat beneath the steering wheel, which meant the intruder either had a key to unlock the vehicle or used a jimmy to open the door. Did he sabotage the vehicle, too?

His attention latched onto a large nail nearby. When he put on a glove and carefully picked it up, he spied bits of red paint on the tip of the nail and dropped it into an evidence bag. Probably nothing would come of it, but near where the nail had been was a piece of gum. It appeared fresh and recently chewed. He also collected it in case DNA could be found on it.

Noting the surveillance camera was still on and active, he hopped back into his car. When Sarah and Candy were safe at his house, he would have her check the footage on her new computer. He didn't think they would get a good photo of whoever defaced Sarah's Chevy, but it had to be checked.

After he called Officer Colby Parker to bring his bomb-sniffing dog to check the car, he drove to the building where the office of Dr. Reichs was and parked as close to the main door as possible. He hoped he'd have a chance to talk to her before Candy was through with her session.

When he entered the reception area for Candy's child psychologist and other professionals in the building, he sought out Sarah, sitting across the room. "Are you all right?"

She glanced up at him, trying to hide her fear and anger. She gave up and said, "No, not at all. The picture of a woman hanging on the side of my car was bad enough, but somehow, he broke into my Chevy so he could place a red carnation on my seat. I always lock my car."

"I'm having your vehicle checked out. When it's cleared, I'll take you to pick it up."

"I'm not safe anywhere."

He sat next to her and took her hand. "I'll bring you to and from work from now on. If I can't, Grandpa will. We'll leave your car in my garage."

"You have a job to do. I can't take you away from that."

"Figuring out what happened at Mary's house to what's going on with you and your secret admirer is my job. Actually, it will make me feel better. I know you didn't want someone driving you to and from work because you wanted your car in case you needed to leave because of an emergency. You might not realize it, but I was following several cars behind you the past few mornings when you went to work. I also tried to get to you before you left, but I wasn't successful yesterday since you left early."

She grinned. "Sorry. I didn't know, or I would have waited for you."

"You never spotted my SUV?"

She shook her head. "I was just watching the car directly behind me. I never claimed to be experienced with the ins and outs of surveillance."

"I'll work with you about being aware of your surroundings at all times. Unless the guy wants you to know he's following you, he'll be watching you from afar."

"Thanks. You've gone above and beyond."

"Just doing my job." Nick glanced at his watch and held his arm up so she could see the time. "Shouldn't Candy be through by now?"

Frown lines cut deep into Sarah's forehead. She bolted to her feet and hurried toward an entrance that led to the clinic offices.

Nick followed quickly and caught up with her as she entered a long hallway with closed doors on both sides. "Are there other ways to get out of this clinic besides the main one?"

"Yes, there's a back door. At the end of this corridor, you turn left and there's an exit." Sarah slowed her pace and a few seconds later came to a stop at a door that had Dr. Emma Reichs on it.

"Does she have a secretary like you?"

"No, this is her office." At the entrance to Emma's office, Sarah knocked. "The six people who work here share a common receptionist and accounting office." Sarah started to rap again when the door swung open. When she saw Candy standing next to the doctor, the tension siphoned from her stance, and she smiled. "How did it go today?" she asked Candy, holding her Teddy bear tightly against her chest.

With her eyes puffy and red, Candy stared at the floor.

Sarah shifted her attention to the child psychologist.

"We're making progress. I'll talk to you later. I have one more person to see in a few minutes." Emma, her expression void of emotions, nodded toward Sarah.

As she took Candy's hand and started for the exit, Nick approached Emma. "Do you have a way to leave your office other than this door?"

"No."

"So, there's only two ways out of here?"

"Yes."

"Thanks." Nick hurried to catch up with Sarah and Candy. With the few things that happened today, he'd decided they needed to be watched more carefully. Candy because her father still hadn't been found and Sarah because someone was trying to frighten her with a threat of killing her. Days ago, Sarah had told him she thought she'd seen Jack Coleman in her rearview mirror in a car right behind her. It was a quick sighting, and she wasn't totally convinced it was him. She was ready to dismiss that she had seen Coleman, while Nick couldn't at all. He hated the feeling he didn't know what was going on. Were the two threats intertwined?

EIGHT

When Sarah's cell phone rang later Wednesday evening, she left the kitchen where the girls were helping Aunt Louise with the cleanup after dinner. As Sarah answered the call, she quickly retreated to the bedroom where she and her aunt slept. "What happened today at your office, Emma?"

"When your aunt brought Candy to the appointment, she wouldn't look up. Louise said the whole way over from school, Candy didn't say a word. She wouldn't talk about what was happening at school as she had on Monday. Even Anna couldn't get her to say anything. After Louise left to take Anna to her ballet class, I tried to get Candy to talk. She didn't say anything for the first forty-five minutes. I tried all kinds of ways to persuade her to talk. Finally, I put a sheet of paper in front of her with colored pencils. Nothing. I began drawing a picture of my family. She picked up a black pencil and started sketching a man."

"Who? Her father?" Sarah sat on the bed.

"I don't know. She wouldn't say anything. Then suddenly when you knocked on my office door, she scribbled over the guy, saying, 'He's here.' Tears ran down her face. She wouldn't move so I started for the door, hoping to get your help. She hopped up and hurried to my side, clasping her arms around me."

"What did she mean by he's here?" Was it Candy's dad?

"She wouldn't say. I tried to get her to tell me, but she wouldn't. I'm on my way home. If you want, I can come to the ranch and see what she'll say now that there has been more time since the man she drew scared her."

"Let me see what she might tell me. Her life has completely changed, and Anna and I are the two constants right now. Can we meet with you tomorrow, preferably after school? I don't want her missing any of her classes. So far, she has been participating in her class some of the time."

"Come at five, after my last patient of the day leaves."

"We'll be there."

As Sarah disconnected her call, a light knock sounded at her bedroom door. When she opened it, she'd hoped it was Candy, but it was Anna instead, forehead crinkled, the corners of her mouth drooping. "What's wrong?"

"Right after you left the kitchen, Candy grabbed her dog and hurried out of the room. I can't find her."

Aunt Louise appeared behind Anna and said, "I can't find her either."

Sarah rose. "Where are Nick and Bernie?"

"Still outside walking around the property. Bella is with Nick."

"Y'all stay in the house. Keep looking for Candy in here. I'm going outside to let Nick know what's going on," Sarah said.

Bella barked. Then again.

The sound sent an alarm clanging through Sarah's body. The words Candy had said, "He's here," urged her to find Nick and let him know. Was *he* here for Candy? Was *he* her father?

Sarah hurried toward the front door. *Please, Lord, protect and heal Candy. I feel lost at how to be there for her. Help me to help her.*

She unlocked the front door and continued out onto the front porch. Her heart thudded against her ribcage. The sound of Bella's barking continued to echo through the darkness. She spied the dog and Nick on the outer reaches of the security lights. His taut stance indicated something or someone was out there. Another coyote or a person here to do harm?

She started to shout to Nick that Candy was missing, but she didn't want to let anyone who might be at the ranch know what was going on. What if Candy left the house and an intruder had captured her? Was that why Bella was barking?

Sarah rushed down the steps and across the yard. Nick glanced over his shoulder toward her. When she reached him, he was facing away from the house as he scanned the dark terrain with night vision goggles. "Candy's missing." She explained what Anna and Aunt Louise had said happened when Candy fled from the kitchen with her puppy. "Why is Bella barking?"

"There was a car at the gate of my

property. She started barking, and I went in that direction. The car drove away."

"How long have you been out front?"

"I came around the side of the house when I heard Bella's first bark. That's when I saw a person. I think it was a woman who opened the driver's side door, climbed into the vehicle, and drove away. I was just about to walk to the gate and check the area."

"A woman?"

"Yes. It's possible she's left an animal at my gate. It won't be the first time that's happened. People know I take in stray animals."

She hoped that was the case. She preferred that rather than someone coming after Candy. "So, you haven't seen Candy?"

"No. Is there any indication she left the house?"

"None other than we haven't found her inside."

"Remember, she's used to hiding and remaining quiet when she feels threatened. I'll let Grandpa know to keep an eye out for her while guarding the yard." Nick called Bernie on his cell phone and explained what happened inside. When he ended the call, Nick started walking toward the porch. "You said she took her puppy. That might help us. Bella's been taught to search for a puppy who's strayed away. Let's see if she can help us find Candy and her pet."

Nick unlocked his front door and entered his home with his dog at his side. "Bella, puppy." His pet sniffed the air then headed toward the kitchen.

Sarah followed her with Nick. "Unless she moved while I was outside, Candy isn't in the kitchen. She left that room when she got upset."

"Let Bella do her thing. She might be going after Anna's Charlie, which is fine. That will rule out one puppy in the house. Then Bella can look in other places for Candy and her pup."

In the kitchen, Anna had put Charlie in her crate for the night. Bella sniffed the puppy and sat. Nick took Charlie out of the crate and held her.

Nick knelt next to Bella and said, "Good dog," while he scratched her behind her ear. He led her out of the kitchen still holding Charlie. "Find the puppy."

Bella took off, smelling the air as Nick went through the house. The second he went into the girls' room, Bella headed for the twin bed, two sides against a wall. Bella crouched low and barked.

Sarah knelt next to Nick's dog and leaned down. Candy held her Teddy bear and her dog against her. The child's eyes, round as saucers, stared at Sarah. How in the world had Candy managed to squeeze under the bed?

"We were so worried about you. Why are you hiding?" Sarah lay flat on the floor and stretched her arms toward Candy. She couldn't cram herself any farther. "You're safe. We've been looking for you. Please, honey, come out. Your puppy is wiggling because she needs to go outside. Nick can take care of that for you."

Candy released her hold on her pet. "Her name is Trixie."

The little girl passed the puppy to Sarah, who gave it to Nick, but the child stayed where she was. "If you aren't coming out, then I'm staying right here." Although talking to Candy, the message was for Nick. She needed to figure out what was going on with the girl. What had frightened her? Who was here in Cimarron City? Where did Candy see the man? The only place she would have seen him today was at school.

After Nick picked up Trixie, he left, shutting the door.

Sarah kept her attention focused on the little girl. Fear carved deep lines into the child's face. "Sweetie, please come out. We can talk sitting on your bed. We'd be more comfortable."

Candy sneezed.

"We've stirred up the dust bunnies. I'll need to clean them out tomorrow." Sarah lifted her hand and hoped that Candy would grasp it. "Please come out, sweetie, and talk to me."

Hesitantly, Candy scooted in her direction and reached toward her. Sarah waited, praying the child would let her help her. Candy grasped Sarah's hand and began slowly to crawl closer to her. When their fingers had touched, she realized that Candy was putting her trust in her.

As they sat on the edge of the bed, Candy hunched her shoulders, bowed her head, and clutched her Teddy bear. Sarah slipped her arm around the six-year-old. "Tell me what happened at school today."

For a long moment, Candy didn't say a word. Her body trembled beneath Sarah's arm. "I can't," came out of the child in a faint whisper.

Sarah drew Candy against her even more. "You said, 'he's here.' Who is he?"

She started to ask if he was her father, but she didn't want to put words into the child's mind that weren't accurate.

"He hurt..."

Again, the minutes ticked away. "You're safe, Candy. You have a lot of us around to protect you. Did the man hurt your mom?"

Candy nodded her head and swiveled around, burying her face into the crook of Sarah's arm so fast it took her by surprise. Sarah embraced the girl, cuddling her as close as she could. The sound of crying, full of pain, came from Candy.

"He hurt her." The words came out in a quivering stream.

On the day of the killing, she'd thought Candy had seen something and possibly even witnessed her mother's murder. "What did he do to hurt your mom?" A shudder flowed through Candy and into Sarah. Her clasp on the child kept her against her side. "I'm not going to let anything happen to you if I have any say in it."

Silence greeted Sarah.

"If you can't tell me, Candy, show me what happened."

The girl kept her head buried against Sarah's side. Minutes passed, and Sarah was afraid she wouldn't say or show her

118

anything. She wasn't ready and might never be.

"It's okay if you don't, Candy."

The six-year-old lifted her head and looked up at Sarah. The color drained from her face. She pulled away and stood next to the bed, her Teddy bear clutched in her right hand while the other was clenched into a fist. She lifted her left hand and stabbed the air over and over, tears rolling down her face.

Sarah rose and drew Candy next to her. "I'm here for you. You can tell me anything. I'll support you. Where did you see him?"

"School when I was leaving."

The quavering in the child's voice tore at Sarah's heart. At least now they knew someone involved in the death of her mother was watching Candy. Was the person her father?

* * *

Nick entered the kitchen to get another cup of coffee. Finally, everyone was asleep after a hectic day. He'd completed his rounds on the ranch and made sure the two kittens, about five or six weeks old that were abandoned at his gate earlier, were settled

119

in the barn with the other animals. He brought the strays back to the house and showed the girls how he fed them with a bottle. When he took the young cats to the barn, he put them in a large cage with bedding and a bowl of water. In the barn, they'd be protected from a bird of prey scooping them up or a coyote catching them outside. Both of the girls had taken to the two kittens right away.

"Is all well at the barn?" Sarah asked as she entered the kitchen.

"You're supposed to be in bed."

"You're kidding. After all that's gone on today." Sarah withdrew a glass from the cabinet, filled it with ice cold water, and took a chair at the table. "I'm glad it was kittens at the gate, not someone after Candy."

"Oh, I don't know. I was ready for a confrontation with the person who killed Mary. Did you find out who Candy said was here?"

"Yes, but she indicated to me that she saw her mother being stabbed by this guy. She didn't tell me, but she showed me this." Sarah went through the motions of striking a person over and over as though holding a knife.

"If she saw the man stabbing her

mother, I can't believe Candy had the sense to get to the safe room and hide."

"When Mary told me about the hidden room, she told me she was doing drills so Candy would go there automatically. At that time, I realized how much Mary feared her ex-husband. I think the man Candy saw was her father although she didn't tell me it was him. My sighting of Jack Coleman tells us he's in town, which means he's probably after his daughter. Mary is dead. Why else would he hang around Cimarron City?"

"Then she needs to stay home from school. Actually, even if it wasn't her father, the man scared her. I agree he's probably her mother's killer."

"I hesitate to keep her from going to school. It's a constant for her. Everything else is new, and a lot of it's terrifying for a six-year-old."

"I've got an idea. I'll pull Officer Landon in to go with Candy to school. She can even take the two girls there and bring them home. That'll give your aunt some relief as well as my grandpa. I know they're both capable of guarding Candy and you, but everyone needs rest to do their best on the job."

Sarah stared at her drink for a long

moment. When she looked up at him, his heartbeat raced. "I'd like Maggie to be in regular clothes, and if the principal and teacher agree, Maggie will be there to help the children like a teacher's aide or a volunteer. Normalcy is important to children, especially Candy."

He smiled. "Actually, it isn't bad for grownups either."

She chuckled. "I've forgotten what that means these past months. The aftermath of the bombings is still affecting quite a few of my patients. At least justice has prevailed in that case."

"And if I have anything to do with it, justice will prevail here too." Nick's gaze bonded with Sarah's. The fatigue in her expression drew him toward her. All he wanted to do was wipe the exhaustion from her face and pull her into his embrace.

Nick started to stand but stopped in mid-action to clasp her hand and cup the side of her face as he drew her to her feet. He brought her close to him and hooked his arm around her. "I won't let anything happen to her. Justice has to prevail."

He lowered his head toward hers, slowly giving her a chance to pull away. There was something about Sarah, a haunting look, that lured him to her. He'd dated, but he always found it was easier to stay at arms' length. He couldn't with Sarah. His lips grazed across hers before he settled his mouth against hers. He didn't want to release her. He became lost in the kiss.

A scream pierced the air.

NINE

Sarah broke away from Nick and whirled about. "That's one of the girls."

He shot ahead of her and raced toward the hallway.

Sarah followed him. He disappeared into Anna's and Candy's bedroom. When she reached the entrance, she nearly ran into his back. Peering around him, Sarah saw Aunt Louise sitting next to Candy, holding the trembling child against her. Anna sat on her bed, her eyes wide as she stared at her friend.

Aunt Louise motioned for Sarah to come forward. She eased down next to Candy and embraced her while her aunt gathered Anna to her side. "She can sleep in our room."

Sarah nodded while Candy clung to her,

her body still quivering as though she was freezing—or scared to death.

After her aunt and Anna left, Nick remained in the doorway.

"Candy, are you all right? Was it a bad dream?"

The little girl nodded her head against Sarah's chest. Candy tightened her grip, making breathing in deeply impossible. Sarah held her a couple of minutes before she drew away, still grasping Candy's upper arms. She looked into the child's eyes. Fear looked back at Sarah.

"What happened? What made you scream? If you have a bad dream, it helps to talk about it." *Before you forget what transpired*.

"He's coming."

"Who? Your dad?"

"Bad man. He's coming for me. He hurt Mom." Tears ran down Candy's face.

"You're safe here." Sarah needed to know who the man was. Her dad?

"He hurt Mom," Candy repeated, her forehead creased.

Sarah wound her arms around the little girl and pressed her against her. "Have you seen him at the ranch too?"

Candy shook her head. Relief fluttered

through Sarah. She hoped that at least the ranch would be a safe haven for the child. How much of Mary's murder had Candy seen? She still hadn't answered if it was her father. Sarah was beginning to think it wasn't the child's dad. In that case, it meant someone else was involved. Alone or with Jack Coleman, who Sarah had seen right before Mary was murdered? She would encourage Candy to draw and paint. Art therapy could be very important for her. Candy had a problem verbally conveying her fears.

Sarah hugged the child against her until Candy closed her eyes and fell asleep. "I've got this, Nick."

"Are you sure?"

"Yes. I'm staying in here with her."

"Okay."

"Close the door but leave the hallway light on."

He nodded and left.

Sarah scooted back against the headboard with Candy next to her and sat up while the girl's head rested in Sarah's lap. Except for a nightlight, the room was dark. She relaxed her tense shoulders and drew in deep, calming breaths.

As a sensation of peace fell over her, a

memory fluttered through her thoughts—the feel of Nick's lips against hers, the sense of security in his embrace, and the musky scent of his aftershave lotion still teasing her nostrils. She was drawn to him even though she didn't want to be. She didn't want to be hurt like that. The remembrance of pulling herself up out of depression after Charlie's death deluged her, as though all of a sudden, she was drowning again in loss and doubt.

How could she ever put herself in that place again? Nick had a dangerous job. If for no other reason, she should keep her emotional distance. She not only needed stability in her life; it was essential for Anna and Candy as well. She prayed that the police would find Mary's murderer.

When sleep began to tug at Sarah, she glanced at Anna's twin bed and decided to move to it. She needed to sleep if she was going to be worth anything tomorrow for her girls and her patients. The second she tried to slip away from Candy, the child burrowed against her, the little girl's arms tightening about Sarah.

She gave up trying to move to the other bed. If Candy woke without her nearby, she might cry out. The child needed her. She was Candy's stability. Sarah adjusted her position so that she was comfortable enough to go to sleep because she had to remain sharp and alert tomorrow.

The one thing they discovered today was that the man who killed Mary was still around and possibly wasn't Candy's dad. Otherwise, why wouldn't Candy say so? If not Jack Coleman, who then would murder Mary, and why? It didn't seem random but personal.

* * *

"Thanks for coming, Colby," Nick said on Saturday as the fellow police officer climbed from his SUV and let his bomb-sniffing dog out of the rear of the vehicle. "I appreciate you and Duke checking out Sarah's car on Wednesday. I wish we had an idea who it was that messed with her Chevy. The camera footage had a blurred image on it. The guy came prepared to keep his identity a secret."

"Any time you need us, call me. You helped me tremendously with the serial bombing case."

Nick kept running into roadblocks on this case, but he would keep chipping away at it.

"With nearly a classroom of kids running around the ranch soon, I know I need help keeping this birthday party safe, especially since the murderer of Candy's mother is still at large."

Colby signaled for Duke to heel. "Are you worried there could be a bomb involved here?"

"No, but then anything is possible. Mainly, I think the kids would love Duke and would love to see how he does his job."

"By sniffing for a bomb for their entertainment?"

Nick chuckled. "Not exactly, but Duke does track people too. Maybe a kid can hide. Then Duke sniffs something belonging to that volunteer. Next he goes and finds the child. I'll demonstrate for the children what a service dog can do, and it'll be fun for them too."

"So, you want Duke to play a hide and seek game with a different twist."

Nick chuckled. "Yup, that about sums it up. When I thought of different ways to keep the kids engaged, he came to my mind. He's a sweet, lovable Rottweiler when he isn't on the job. And not to mention, Bella has missed him."

"This can be a great opportunity to show

your party-goers what a special K-9 can do. What other games do you have for the children?"

"I have several horses gentle enough for them to ride in a corral. Especially one is really gentle with first time riders. And in another corral, the kids can race around barrels, if they're experienced enough to do that. Also, for the ones who can't rope an animal, I'll show them how with a wooden cow. That's my part while Sarah and Louise will have other games and activities under the tent." Nick glanced into the SUV's front seat. "Where's your wife? Sarah was looking forward to seeing Beth. Isn't she helping Sarah?"

"Yes, she's coming." Colby's gaze swept the area. "How many children will be here?"

"Everyone in Candy's class was invited, but I think Sarah said that fifteen are coming. There were a few who couldn't make it."

"How's Candy doing?"

"This has been a rocky week. Most of the time she's quiet. Sarah's trying to get her to talk more. She hardly speaks even at school with her friends. The one good thing about being here are the animals. Candy loves them. In fact, Sarah caught the child talking to her puppy, but Sarah could only catch a few words of what she said."

"And still no idea where Candy's father is?"

Nick sighed. "He's disappeared in Houston. The police there have interviewed many people, but no one knows where he is—or rather, no one will tell us where he went. Then when Sarah went to pick up Anna and Candy, she believes she saw him at school on the Tuesday before the fall break, two days before Mary was murdered. Sarah didn't realize Coleman was here until I showed her a photo of the guy. She hadn't seen one before that. No sightings other than that since then."

Anna ran up to Nick. "I can't find Candy."

Nick stiffened. The children would start arriving in the next fifteen or twenty minutes. "Where did you see her last?"

"In the barn with Bella, Trixie, and the new kittens. I ran to the house to get Charlie, and when I came back, she was gone."

"I'll take care of it. Let your mom know."

"Okay." Anna ran toward the house.

"Do you have something of Candy's that Duke can smell?"

"I'll be right back." Nick jogged toward

his house. "Bella, come," Nick called out in case his dog was nearby.

When Bella didn't come to him, he shouted her name again even louder, adding Candy's too. Still no Bella or Candy. That meant his dog wasn't in the vicinity. Were the two together? Candy and Trixie were inseparable. Where was her puppy? Since the child had arrived at the ranch, Bella had been extra protective of Candy, as though the sorrow had drawn his pet to the girl.

Inside his home, Nick went to the girls' bedroom and grabbed a shirt Candy wore yesterday then started for the front door.

Sarah stopped him before he put his hand on the knob. "Candy's missing! Anna just told me."

"I told her to let you know. When was the last time you saw her?"

"She left the kitchen a while ago to get dressed. Bella was with her. Candy seemed excited her friends were coming to her birthday party. She wasn't supposed to go outside without letting me know." Sarah glanced at the clock on the wall. "That was twenty minutes ago. I've been so busy I didn't realize she'd been gone that long."

"Don't blame yourself. Kids can lose sense of time. Have you looked around in here?"

"We will." Sarah's gaze latched onto the shirt in his hand. "Are you going to try to find her with Bella?"

"I don't know where Bella is. She and Trixie are both gone as well. I think they might be with Candy. Duke's here. Colby's going to have Duke search for her. We're starting in the barn since that's the last place Anna saw Candy."

"I'll be outside as soon as we've checked the house, especially under Candy's bed."

Nick made his way to the entry hall, Candy's shirt in hand, and opened the front door. "Hopefully, the two are together. Go ahead and check the house. I'll take care of the rest. I have my cell phone. Call if you find her, and I'll do the same."

As he made his way back to Colby, he wished that Candy wouldn't vanish without notifying one of them where she was going. Probably the little girl was fine, but it would only take one time for someone to snatch her when she was alone. And with the killer as well as her father still out there, she was at risk. Sarah thought that Candy had seen the murderer and could identify him. The child was drawing a man in black with extra details added with each picture she provided.

"This is Candy's shirt." Nick handed Colby the piece of clothing and started for the barn." When he entered the building, his grandfather was putting a saddle on one of the horses for the kids to ride. "Have you seen Candy? She was in here not long ago."

"Nope, but then I just arrived after getting the barrels set up in the corral for the kids. Is she hiding again?"

"I hope that's all it is. Duke's going to track her."

"You know I haven't seen Bella lately. She isn't with you?" Grandpa set the saddle on the back of a mare.

"Bella was in the house when Candy was, but both are gone." While Colby held the shirt out for Duke to smell, Nick stepped to the double front doors and shouted, "Come, Bella." When he glanced over his shoulder and saw the Rottweiler sniff the air then head out the back of the barn, Nick looked forward and spied a car coming down the driveway toward the house. "Grandpa, I need you to see to the people starting to arrive."

"Sure. You go and find Candy. I'll take care of things here."

Nick jogged out the rear exit, caught

sight of Colby and Duke, and closed the distance to them. When he reached Colby following behind Duke a couple of yards. Nick's cell phone rang.

"Have you found Candy? The children are arriving," Sarah said, her fear conveyed in the tightness in her voice.

"I think Duke's homing in on her." A yelp echoed through the woods. "Bella's barking. We're near. I'll call you back when I see her."

Nick ran beside Colby toward the noise. In the midst of Bella's yapping, a deep bark resonated through the trees.

"Duke's there." Colby increased his strides.

Nick followed, assessing his surroundings. From the sounds of the dogs, they had to be on the rear edge of the woods where a dirt road ran. Overriding questions wouldn't shake loose from his mind. What would draw Candy to that area, and why would she go there alone?

Unless someone—possibly the killer or her father—took her or lured her there. His police instinct took over. What if this was a trap?

The trees became denser, the slope of the land about thirty degrees with the road at the bottom.

As Nick grew closer, the barking subsided. He caught sight of Candy lying on the ground, and his heart sank. He ran down the slope, glimpsing Trixie curled against the young girl, the pup's brown eyes glued to him. As Nick stooped next to the child, her eyes fluttered open. He gently took the puppy from her arms and handed her to Colby.

"Are you all right?" Nick ran his gaze down her length.

"My foot caught on something." She slowly pushed herself to a sitting position then held her arms out toward Colby. "Is Trixie okay?" Pieces of leaves lay trapped in Candy's long hair.

"Yes." Colby passed the puppy to her.

"Do you think you can stand?" Nick asked, only seeing a few scratches on her legs and arms. It could have been a lot worse. He reached out and assisted her to her feet. "Okay?"

She nodded.

Nick withdrew his cell phone and called Sarah. "We found her. We'll be back in a few minutes. She went down a slope the fast way and needs to clean up.

"Just so she's okay." Relief flowed

through Sarah's voice.

"See you soon." Nick disconnected the call and returned his attention to Candy. "Why did you come out here?"

Candy hung her head and stared at her feet. "I was scared. Trixie disappeared. I wasn't paying attention to her. I was playing with the kittens. I gave Bella the command to find Trixie. Then I followed Bella."

"Scared about what?"

"Trixie being lost. I should have paid more attention to her in the barn."

"Let's go back. The party's going to start soon." Nick held his hand out for Candy.

She didn't take it and instead dropped her head. "I don't think anyone is coming to my party. No one is talking to me except Anna at school. They whisper behind my back."

Nick squatted. "It can be hard, especially for children, to figure out what to say to you. I know when I left to find you, I saw a couple of cars already coming down the driveway."

"You did?"

He nodded. "You should see all the cool things set up for you and your friends. Horse rides. Learning to rope a cow. Games to play. Anna and Sarah wanted you to have a nice birthday. A lot of people care about you."

Tears flooded her eyes. "I want my mom."

Nick didn't know what to say or do. This was Sarah's territory. "I know you do. She's looking down on you from Heaven and loving you. Your mom will always be with you in your heart."

"Why did he kill her?"

"Who?"

"The bad man."

"You never saw him before that day?"

"No."

"But you saw him in your house and later outside your school?"

Candy swiped her fingers across her cheeks. "Yes."

"What did he look like?"

"Big. Mean."

"Not your dad?"

"No."

"If you saw him again, would you recognize him?"

Her top teeth worried her lower lip, and she nodded. "I won't forget his face."

Nick wished he could pursue this topic, but Candy needed to see how much her classmates cared about her. As they walked back through the woods, Nick went over what Candy told him. If the assailant in her house wasn't the little girl's father, then why did Coleman come to Cimarron City before Mary's murder? Could it be possible her dad hired someone to kill Mary? He would be the prime suspect, so why wasn't he trying to establish an alibi in Texas the day Mary was killed? Instead, he was probably here which wouldn't help his case. So many questions and no answers.

A prickle ran up and down Nick's spine. He glanced over his shoulder, and for a second, he thought he saw a glint coming from the woods on the other side of the dirt road.

TEN

Sarah watched the last car with two of Anna's and Candy's classmates leaving the ranch. As she leaned against a porch post, she released a long breath and closed her eyes, the cool breeze brushing across her face, bringing the scent of the outdoors in the autumn. Candy had been timid at first, but as more and more of her friends showed up, she began to blossom and ended up smiling ear to ear. She'd enjoyed herself and relaxed for a couple of hours. Sarah had wanted Candy to see how much others cared about her.

Anna and Candy came out of the barn with their puppies in their arms and headed toward the house. Sarah needed to talk to Candy about leaving and not letting them know—but not until later because the child desperately needed to realize she wasn't alone. Sarah would be there for her.

"You two look tired," she said as the girls mounted the steps to the porch.

Anna and Candy glanced at each other, and they both nodded at the same time.

Sarah smiled, chalking up the day as a success. "I know how you feel. I'm going to bed early tonight."

Anna stopped. "Not us. Remember, you told us we could stay up 'til midnight on our birthdays."

"Oh, I forgot. If you two can, that's fine."

Candy yawned, which immediately caused both Anna and her to do the same. Sarah's grin grew as the girls went inside. She suspected they would be asleep by eight or nine o'clock. They headed inside while Sarah remained on the porch.

As the sun began its descent on the western horizon, Nick and Bernie exited the barn, closing the double doors. When they reached the porch, Nick's granddad continued walking into the house while Nick stayed, leaning back against the wooden railing, his arms crossed.

"I assume Anna and Candy went inside." Nick pushed his western hat up on his forehead.

"Yes. They're worn out," Sarah said. "I don't think they're going anywhere tonight."

"But how about tomorrow?" Nick unfolded his arms and gripped the railing on both sides of him.

"We need to give her a place to go when she feels threatened."

"Yeah. I know she went after Trixie earlier, but she has to realize she can't leave without letting us know."

"I wanted to do the birthday party to help her see how many people care about her and to take her mind off what had happened last week. Every night she's had a nightmare. She's afraid she'll be left alone. I reassured her she's part of my family now— that we'll be going to court to make it official soon." Sarah turned toward Nick. "Mary taught her daughter when she became afraid to flee to the safe room in the house. That's been her way of dealing with any sense of danger or fear in the past year."

"So, that's why she's fleeing and hiding whenever something concerns her?"

"Yes. But I'll need to teach her another way to deal with fear. She needs to learn when to do it and when not to flee and hide."

"Candy told me her dad wasn't the person who killed her mother."

"Are you going to stop looking for Mary's ex-husband?"

"No. He could have hired someone, or he could have been there, but Candy didn't see him. Or she could be denying he was in their home. The question I keep asking myself is what's the motive for an unknown person to kill Mary other than Coleman paying him. The murder isn't similar to the ones we've had in the past year in Cimarron City. There wasn't a robbery at least of the obvious items a person might take. According to the people who knew Mary, they couldn't understand why anyone would want to kill her. You were the one who gave me the information about her ex-husband. He had a motive, and you saw him in Cimarron City before the murder was committed. From what I've discovered about the missing man, he had unsavory connections, people who've spent time in prison." Nick pushed himself away from the railing and faced Sarah.

"He does? Mary didn't say anything about his acquaintances."

"She might not have known about them." Nick took her hands and closed the small space between them.

"I'll feel better when you find Mary's ex-husband as well as the killer, if he didn't murder her. With the uncertainty of where her father is, it'll be hard for Candy ever to have closure about her mother's death."

"Hopefully, the memorial service for her mother after church tomorrow will be a step forward for Candy."

"Emma will be attending. I'll let her know what happened today, especially what Candy told you." His nearness sent her heartbeat pounding through her body. The feel of his hands cupping hers gave her a sense of peace. She wasn't alone in dealing with what was occurring all around her. "I probably shouldn't have planned a birthday party for Candy. It was too soon."

"She really enjoyed learning to ride Sadie. She told me she'd never been on a horse. At first, she was scared, but after going around the corral once, she smiled the rest of the time. I told her I would let her ride whenever she wanted so long as Grandpa or I was there to help her. I also told Anna the same thing."

"Anna has always loved horses, and getting to ride one earlier made her day, too."

"Good. I'm going to start teaching them

how to take care of the horse they ride. Like with their puppy, it helps them to feel good about themselves. I've seen it with both girls." Nick released her hands and combed his fingers through her long blond hair that cascaded about her shoulders.

The sensations his touch produced in her flooded her system. Her legs weakened, and she grasped his shoulders to steady herself.

He closed the space between them even more and dipped his head toward her. His lips brushed across hers, causing her grip on his shoulders to tighten to keep her upright. When his mouth covered hers, she surrendered to the sensations he created in her—a warm cozy bliss that wrapped her in a cocoon of protection. His arms embraced her as he deepened the kiss. For a moment, she could forget the trials of the past ten days.

The sound of giggles penetrated her hazy mind. She slanted a glance toward the front door and quickly stepped away from Nick as the heat of embarrassment flamed her face.

Both Candy and Anna covered their mouths with their hands as they continued to laugh.

"Did you need something?" Sarah asked as she headed toward them.

Anna shook her head. "Aunt Louise said dinner's ready."

"Okay. I'll be right there. Go wash your hands."

They whirled around and raced away.

Nick walked toward her, snagged her with his arm, and drew her against him. His quick kiss left her dazed and wanting more, but he released her and continued toward the entrance. Sarah followed, beginning to prepare for the interrogation she'd go through tonight with Anna and Candy.

* * *

The next day after the memorial service for Mary, Nick parked in front of his house. The whole way back to his ranch silence had ruled. He didn't know what he should do to make the day better for Candy. She hadn't said a word since the memorial service. As Nick climbed from his SUV, Grandpa pulled up behind him with Louise in his truck. The second his granddad turned his engine off, he was out the door and scurried around the hood to open the passenger door. He offered Louise his hand as she stepped down. Nick's eyes widened at the sight. Was something going on between Grandpa and Louise?

He'd been so concentrated on keeping Candy, Anna, and Sarah safe that Nick hadn't seen a connection developing between his grandfather and Sarah's aunt. He remembered they had sat next to each other at church and later during the memorial service, but Nick had kept his attention focused on the people who had attended, mostly from the church and where Mary had worked at International Food, Inc. He couldn't help but wonder if the killer had attended the service. It wouldn't be the first time that happened. He'd prepared himself for all kinds of situations today because killers in the past have gone to their victim's funeral.

The girls ran toward the porch with Louise and Grandpa following behind them while Sarah hung back.

Nick joined her. "Are you all right?"

"It's been a long day."

"Candy seemed to handle herself well."

"She barely looked up and was withdrawn, which is to be expected. I spoke with Emma, and she'll be seeing Candy after school tomorrow." Sarah started toward the house.

Nick fell into step with her, his gaze drawn to the porch where Anna held a vase of flowers. There had been many bouquets at the memorial service that were left to go to people in nursing homes and the hospital. His gut tightened. Her stalker had come to his ranch.

Sarah slowed her steps. A few yards away, she came to a stop. "They're black carnations."

Louise took the vase from Anna. "I'll take care of these."

His granddad unlocked the door and with the two girls right behind him, hurried inside to turn off the alarm system. Sarah's aunt stayed back.

Nick took Sarah's hand and cut the distance between them and Louise. "Don't touch anything else." He hurried to his car, pulled out two latex gloves from a box and retrieved evidence bags. He always kept these things inside his SUV just in case. Then he returned. "Let me take them. They're evidence."

Louise gave the vase with its grim carnations to him. "There's a note." She nodded her head at the back of the flowers where a small white card was nestled among the carnations.

Nick didn't know if any fingerprints could be found that would lead to the stalker, but he was going to try to minimize the contamination of the evidence. He removed the flowers and dumped the water from the vase. Then he lifted the card from the holder and placed the flowers and the vase in separate bags. He opened the card. "It reads, 'Where have you been?'"

Louise frowned. "What's that supposed to mean?"

Sarah shook her head. "I'm more concerned about the color of the carnations. A definite shift from bright colors to black."

Louise released a long breath and headed inside.

Sarah sank onto the porch swing, hugging her arms against her chest.

Nick sat next to her and put the card into its own evidence bag. "I'll see if I can get fingerprints off the piece of paper. I'll need Louise's to compare with any on the vase or card. It'll be obvious where Anna held the vase."

Sarah's shoulders drooped forward. "It must be one of my clients. With all that's occurred, I've had to shuffle appointments and even cut some of the time I see a few of my patients."

"Possibly or maybe it's because you aren't at your home."

"But the person knows where I am because he left the bouquet on your porch. I guess he followed me to find where I went."

"That doesn't mean he isn't upset you aren't at your house."

"This clinches it. I have a stalker. I didn't want to admit it. I've worked with troubled people, but I've never been scared one would come after me. Why now in the middle of all this?"

"It started before Mary's murder." Sitting next to Sarah, Nick felt the shudder rippling down her length. "He's a stalker. Leaving flowers, possibly involved in your office break-in. He broke into your car. He was a threat from the beginning. I've dealt with people like this during my career. It usually builds up until he snaps."

Sarah's eyes widened as he talked. "I'd put this out of my mind, focusing on Candy. Since we came here, this has been the first time we've all been gone from your ranch. That's when the person struck. Do you think he's been watching the whole time and waiting for his opportunity?"

"Maybe. It wasn't a secret we'd be at Mary's memorial service." Nick rose. "Let's go inside. I need to check the security cameras."

"You have cameras around here."

"Yes. I put them in right before you came. They aren't obvious, and hopefully, the person who left the vase didn't see them."

As they entered the house, Sarah said, "I'm going to see how the girls are doing."

"I'll be in my office checking the camera feeds." He didn't tell her he would also be looking at the footage at the barn and inside his house. It didn't appear the assailant came into his home, but he always considered all possibilities.

The first video he pulled up was at the entrance to the ranch. He had a gate that remained shut and locked when he was gone. Nothing appeared on the camera. So, probably whoever delivered the black carnations must have climbed over the fence, most likely from the back of the property off the paved road that ended at a small lake.

He continued going through the footage and finally spied a person. In Nick's estimation, he was of medium height. His build was thin, and by his bearing and strides, probably a male. He wore a brown ski mask. As he zoomed in on one shot from a hidden camera near the intruder, Nick enlarged the picture of someone with bright blue eyes. Not much to go on, but he hoped there were fingerprints on the note and the vase that would help him identify the intruder. Using various cameras, he tracked the man's path, coming from the rear along the road behind his property. A camera on his deck had caught the best images. He printed the picture then blew up the words on his jacket—IFI, a company for the future, the one where Mary worked. He ran off that photo too.

When he finished studying the footage, Nick stood and went into the kitchen. "Do you have an idea where black carnations are sold? I've never seen that color for them," he asked Louise.

"Carnations can be dyed a certain color. Those were a bad dye job. It looked like he bought white ones which are common and turned them black."

"So, time and thought went into this. The intruder came from the rear of my ranch. I'm going to try to find a set of footprints from the boots he wore and see if I can tell exactly where he came from."

Armed with his handgun, Nick called Bella then set out to see if he could find the path the guy had taken to the house. There was a gentle rain last night, so there might be something. He needed a break.

Remembering how the guy appeared on the camera, coming toward the back of his house from the left, he headed that way. He paused at a set of footprints that could be the intruder's, took a photo of the area, and let Bella sniff the ground. He'd been working with her to follow a scent, and she had proved to be a quick learner. The impression of the boot indicated the man put more pressure on the inside of his left foot. Nick climbed over his back fence, crossed the paved road, and entered the trees to follow Bella, which meant the intruder might have parked farther away, possibly on the dirt road on the other side of the woods.

The trail the trespasser had taken was easier to see once he went into the thick woods where the ground was mostly bare. As he moved among the trees right behind Bella, he kept sweeping the terrain around him. When he reached the edge of the woods between the paved road and the dirt one behind his ranch, he spied tire tracks in the muddy ground. With his dog beside him, he squatted down where the footprints were and took photos of them and the tire tracks, which showed the driver had made a U-turn.

This road was more isolated and a better place for the intruder to park his car and head to Nick's ranch.

When he stood, he looked down the dirt lane in the direction of the highway. Tomorrow he would check to see if there were live traffic cams on the highway. It was a longshot, but he didn't have a lot to go on. Then he glanced in the opposite direction toward the campground, not far from the lake, at the end of the lane.

His gaze swept the terrain around him. A glint coming from the other side of the road deep in the woods along the lake attracted his attention. He decided to check it out. It would be too far away to watch the ranch, but maybe someone wanted to hide his means of getting away. He might still be hanging around, hiding in the thick undergrowth in certain places.

He made a call to his granddad and told him what he was doing. "I need you to stay with them in the house. Don't let anyone leave until I check this out."

He disconnected with Grandpa and headed toward the area. As he drew closer, he could make out a black vehicle that someone had put leafy branches over as though that would camouflage the car. He approached the vehicle with no license plate cautiously with his gun in his hand and Bella at his side.

A sickeningly ripe odor assaulted his nostrils.

ELEVEN

Sarah entered the girls' bedroom at Nick's house and found Candy asleep. She stood in the entrance watching the child. Her heart felt as though it swelled in her chest. She knew personally what it was like to mourn someone close. Her mother died ten years ago, followed by Charlie five years later. She was thankful that Anna never had to go through that pain at a young age because she was only a one year old when her father passed away. Sarah had been an adult and was blindsided both times. With support and the Lord, she'd managed to deal with each death.

Lord, please help Candy through this tragedy. Show me what I need to do besides loving her. I know time helps, but only if she has a firm foundation and people who care about her.

It was one thing that she had a stalker. She would deal with it, but Candy was only a child, and she had someone after her. Why? For days, the same question assaulted her thoughts. Why go after Candy?

Bernie came down the hall and stopped by her. "We need to talk."

She followed him into Nick's office. When Bernie closed the door, she knew something was wrong. His facial features tightened into a frown from his slashed eyebrows to his tense thin lips. "What happened? Where's Nick?"

"He's in the woods. He thinks someone might be watching the house."

"My stalker?"

"Probably since the footprints Nick was following were from the man who left the vase. At least that's what he thinks."

"Then at least Candy's safe."

"We don't know what's going on. Everyone needs to stay in the house. The alarm system is on, and I've checked all the doors and windows. If anyone tries to come inside or leave the house, we'll know. I've told Louise. She's with Anna in the kitchen right now. They're working on dinner."

Bernie headed into the hallway. Sarah approached the window that faced toward the rear of the property. What was going on? It seemed every day something occurred concerning Candy's safety as well as her own. Already Sarah felt like a she-bear trying to protect her cub.

She started to leave and glanced down at the couch against the wall. She picked up the blanket on the cushion, folded it, then placed it on the pillow. Since she and Aunt Louise were in Nick's bedroom, this was where he slept while they were here.

He had told her once that his ranch was his sanctuary, a place he went to unwind and decompress. His job took its toll on him. He'd seen more than his share of evil and tragedy. When he'd invited her and her family to stay here, he'd given up a lot and had never indicated he wanted it any other way.

She touched her lips, and for a few seconds, she remembered his kiss yesterday—and cherished it. She'd wanted it to continue. She hadn't realized how much she missed that connection with a man, especially someone like Nick, a godly man with integrity and compassion. Charlie would have liked him.

She shook her head. She had so much to deal with right now. Why in the world was she fantasizing about a man who had remained single all his life? One who had a dangerous job?

She swept around and hurried from the room. What in the world was she thinking? That she and Nick could have a relationship? No, she had two little girls she had to put first. They depended on her.

Sarah peeked into the bedroom where Candy still slept, clutching her Teddy bear against her chest as though it were her life preserver while Trixie was stretched out against Candy's back. She was flanked by the two things that gave her comfort in the middle of the chaos of her life right now.

When Sarah entered the kitchen, she smelled the scent of dinner, her aunt's spaghetti. Her sauce, from an Italian relative, was delicious. The scent of onions, tomatoes, peppers, and various spices overrode all other smells in the house. "My mouth is already watering. How long will it be until dinner?"

Aunt Louise glanced at the wall clock. "In an hour."

Anna groaned. "I'm hungry now."

Sarah put her hand on her daughter's

shoulder. "Tell you what. Why don't you get a piece of fruit to tide you over until we eat?"

"How about ice cream instead? It won't ruin my dinner."

"You can have ice cream after you eat your meal."

Anna wrenched herself away from her and stomped her foot. "If Candy wanted ice cream, she would get it."

Before Sarah could say anything, her daughter raced from the room, nearly running into Bernie coming through the doorway. He stepped quickly out of the way.

She found Anna in the den where she'd thrown herself on a couch, her face turned away from Sarah. She sat on the edge of the leather sofa. "This isn't about you having ice cream. What's going on, Anna? I know it's been crazy lately, but everything will settle down." At least Sarah prayed it would.

Anna didn't say anything.

"What Candy's going through is very hard on anyone, especially a child. She needs your friendship and support as well as mine. I know I've been spending more time with her lately, but she just lost her mother and needs help. She needs someone to listen to her and show her she isn't alone.

You've been doing a good job doing exactly that. I hope you'll continue. Do you think you can?"

After a long moment, Anna rolled over, looking up at Sarah. "I will. What's going on?"

Sarah brushed her daughter's hair away from her cheek. "I don't know for sure. But we're safe here until we find out. I thought you were enjoying staying here."

"I am, but I'm scared. I wanted to go to the barn to see the kittens and to the corral to see the horses. I'd like to ride one again, but Aunt Louise said I had to stay in the house."

"You and Candy will get to go back to the barn at some point." Sarah clasped Anna's hand. "I want you to know that I'll be adopting Candy. She'll be part of our family. Her mother asked me to be her daughter's guardian if anything happened to her. I agreed, especially because you two were such good friends and because I feel we should help others whenever we can."

"Candy's going to be my sister?"

"Yes."

"Good. I've always wanted one."

"Don't say anything to her yet. I'll let you know when you can. Okay?"

Anna nodded. "I'm still hungry. Can I have a little ice cream?"

"Not until after dinner. Then you can eat all you want. Don't forget the apple is still—"

"No! No!" Candy screamed.

* * *

Nick tossed the leafy branches away from the abandoned car and peered into its interior. Empty. The nauseating scent that drifted to him churned his stomach. The stench screamed that a dead animal or person was nearby. After he slipped on the gloves he'd used earlier, he opened the driver's door to pop the trunk then rounded the rear to lift it.

Nick stared at Jack Coleman crammed into the car's trunk. He'd been killed by a gunshot to the heart. Nick wouldn't know how long Mary's ex-husband had been dead until the medical examiner arrived. The odor coming from the body indicated it could have been around twenty-four hours ago or longer. The medical examiner would be able to narrow the time, taking into consideration the temperature. Without moving the body, he inspected the area around the body and found nothing.

He withdrew his cell phone from his pocket and took several photos of the dead body. Then he placed a call to headquarters to report the death of Jack Coleman and requested a team to deal with the crime scene. He didn't want to be gone from the house for too long. He made another call to his grandpa to make sure everything was okay.

"I found Jack Coleman dead in a trunk of a Ford Fiesta. I asked headquarters for a canine team to follow the scent of the driver when he dumped the car and left."

"You want to know if the killer came to your ranch?"

"Yes," Nick said as he thought about having Bella try to follow the scent too. She was being trained and was doing well, but he wanted another canine to support what happened. Too many people he cared about were at stake. As soon as a police officer arrived, he would turn the crime scene over to him and hightail it back to his house. "I know the scent will vanish when the driver gets into another vehicle, but where is that? I'll be back as soon as possible."

"I'll let Sarah know Coleman's dead."

"See you soon."

Nick disconnected the call and moved to

the car's interior to see what evidence he could find. He didn't have evidence bags, but he'd point out to the police what he wanted bagged up and processed. As he combed through the vehicle, he couldn't stop thinking about the case and the questions filling his mind, but one dominated his thoughts.

Who killed Jack Coleman, and why?

* * *

"Don't!"

The sound of the scream propelled Sarah to her feet. "Anna, go into the kitchen and tell Bernie I need him."

Sarah hurried down the hall to the girls' bedroom and came to a halt just inside. Candy held a wiggling Trixie. "Is something wrong?"

"She tried to jump down to the floor." Candy hugged the puppy close to her chest. "She could have hurt herself."

Sarah didn't respond for a few seconds because her heartbeat had skyrocketed. The tension around her was palpable. "Maybe she needs to go to the bathroom."

The little girl's eyes widened. "I need to take her outside."

Nick's granddad appeared next to Sarah and slipped his handgun into his pocket. "Everything's fine here?"

Sarah nodded. "Candy, Bernie will take Trixie outside."

She scooted to the edge of the bed and stood with her puppy in her hands. "I want to."

Sarah drew in a deep breath. "Not right now. Maybe later we'll go to the barn. Wait until Nick comes back."

"Where did he go?" Candy asked.

"Into the woods checking out something. Why don't you go into the kitchen and help Aunt Louise with dinner? Anna is in there."

"Okay." Candy passed Trixie to Bernie then headed for the kitchen.

"Walk with me outside," Bernie said as he turned and started down the hallway.

By his demeanor, she could see something was wrong. What was it? "We shouldn't be gone long."

"I agree." Bernie turned off the alarm, stepped outside onto the front porch, and descended to the ground. After putting Trixie on the grass, he pivoted toward her. "Nick called me a few minutes ago. He found an abandoned car with Jack Coleman dead in the trunk."

"Mary's ex-husband was behind this house in the woods?"

"Yes."

"How long?"

"Don't know."

"Why was he here? To kidnap Candy? What's going on? Who killed him and why?"

TWELVE

Nick and Bella approached the rear of his house. When he reached his patio, the back door opened, and Sarah slipped outside.

"Where was he?" she asked and closed the distance between them.

As Bella sat next to Nick, he pointed in the direction slightly to the right. "There's a paved road that goes to the lake behind my property, but beyond that about a fourth of a mile away there's a dirt road that the couple who run the campground put in for people who come to their place. An old black Ford Fiesta was left about thirty yards away from the road on the other side. It was covered with branches. Coleman was in the trunk, shot in the heart. A forensics team is processing the car and the area right now. Probably whoever drove the car and left it there had someone on the dirt road waiting to take the driver away."

Sarah paled. "Why leave it there?"

"A message possibly. It's common knowledge the police are searching for Jack Coleman as a person of interest in Mary's murder."

"What if there was more than one person who broke into Mary's house? Killing her and trashing those two bedrooms would take some time. One could have murdered her while another was searching for whatever they were looking for. But then what was the guy searching for in the bedrooms? Candy or something else?

"Good questions. I've been thinking it was Candy because I thought the killer was Coleman. He disappeared a few days before Mary was murdered and turned up here. That would give him time to case the location of where Mary lived and follow her movements."

"Could her ex-husband have brought a partner? Being in prison, he could have met an unsavory guy who would help him get revenge since Mary called the police on him." Sarah raked her hand through her hair and hooked the strands behind her ears.

"I've been going back and forth about whether there was one person or two. The fingerprints didn't show anyone except Mary and Candy had been there."

"Mary had people over to her house, including Anna and me, but she kept her house spotless, so I can see why no other fingerprints showed up."

"There were a few different children's prints in Candy's room, but I didn't want to waste my time pursuing them." Nick looked toward the rear double doors and spied Anna and Candy pressed against the glass, both longingly staring at them. "We have two munchkins watching us."

"Yeah, I told them we would go to the barn when you came back."

"We'll talk more later. I don't want to disappoint them. Today was tough for Candy. Let's take her mind off the memorial service and make her smile."

"Maybe taking her mind off all that has happened for the rest of the day might refresh us enough so that we can figure out what happened."

Nick grasped Sarah's hand and threaded his fingers through hers. "Good suggestion." He covered the distance to the door.

The girls didn't move. Anna lifted her chin and looked at her mom. "We're ready to go to the barn."

Sarah smiled. "Sounds good. I'll tell Aunt Louise and Bernie." Candy quickly stepped away to let her come inside.

After Sarah disappeared from view, Nick signaled for the girls to come outside. Both of them made a beeline to Bella and petted her. His dog licked Candy's face, and she giggled. Bella loved people, but she especially was drawn to ones who were hurting. She knew what Candy needed. She'd done the same to him when he'd been hurting and struggling from his near death.

"Are you two up for riding? We're going to get both of them ready to ride. Who's riding Tilly?"

Anna raised her arm.

"Then, Candy, you can ride Sadie."

Candy pumped her arm into the air. Grins from ear to ear appeared on their faces.

Anna glanced over her shoulder at the door then started toward it. "What's taking Mom so long?"

"She'll be here in a minute. She still had on her dress and heels. She probably wanted to change before going to the barn."

Anna drifted back to Nick and Candy. A few seconds later, Sarah appeared at the door.

"It's about time, Mom." Anna took her hand and tugged her forward.

Nick chuckled. "I think two girls want to go riding."

"You think!" Some of the tension that had been in Sarah's face was gone.

Anna and Candy ran ahead of them with Bella staying at their side.

"I asked Aunt Louise to hold dinner so the girls can have a couple of hours with the animals."

The two mares trotted around the corral nearest the barn. Tilly came to the fence first. Anna stuck her arm through the slats to pet her. When Candy arrived, she climbed halfway up the fence and called out to Sadie. The blond five-year-old mare immediately headed for Candy.

The child twisted toward Sarah. "She knows me!" Sadie nudged Candy, and she laughed.

The sound from her was beautiful for Nick to hear. He knew how much animals could help people overcome pain and sorrow. In Cimarron City, there were other children who needed a place to go and interact with animals. For the past few months, as more abandoned pets were left at his gate or were given to him, he'd been thinking about doing something with the animals he had at the ranch. Seeing Candy's reaction to Sadie and Trixie cemented that mission for him. Now, he just had to figure out what and how to do it.

"What are you thinking?" Sarah asked, pulling his attention to her.

He turned to her and smiled. "I don't know at this time. Maybe when the case is over, I'll have time to look at what I could do with my abandoned animals to help others."

"I know of an organization in town you might team up with. Pals works with children who are disadvantaged. It isn't just economically but emotionally disadvantaged kids who don't have a mother, father, or a sibling. Emma works with the group."

"I'll get in touch with her."

"Can we ride?" Candy asked as she climbed down from the fence.

"Yes. I'll go and bring out the saddles. Both of you can learn how to put one on."

The girls beamed.

"We'll help you." Anna started for the barn.

Nick headed after Candy and Anna. Having the two girls here at his ranch helped clarify what he'd been thinking about for the past year. It gave a spring to his steps. When Sarah came up to his side and walked with him, the urge to clasp her hand and pull her close to his side filled him. He cared about her and that thought concerned him. He'd dated and even became serious when he first was a police officer. But his job had always gotten in the way. Finally, he'd decided to devote himself to one or the other. His job won out because he loved aiding people, especially in times like the past bombing spree or what was going on with Sarah and Candy. He needed to back away emotionally.

* * *

Later that night after dinner, Sarah sat in the den with everyone for a game of charades. Anna and Bernie were on her team.

"We won!" Candy pumped her arm in the air.

The grins on Nick's and Aunt Louise's faces matched the little girl's.

"We need to do another game." Bernie

yawned. "Maybe just as soon as I take a nap."

Aunt Louise chuckled. "Not gonna happen tonight. Tomorrow is a school day."

Bernie rose and called Bella to him. "First let's take your dogs outside."

Both of the children scooped up their pets and headed for the rear door.

Aunt Louise picked up the tray with a few leftover chocolate chip cookies, placed the empty glasses on it, and headed into the kitchen.

Although Bernie was with the girls, Sarah crossed the room to the double back doors to watch them as the darkness crept over the terrain. The security lights illuminated a good part of the yard. But she couldn't forget what had been discovered a short distance from this house.

Nick approached her. "They're okay. Bella will let us know if someone's out there. She's a great watchdog. Besides, Bernie is so invested in the girls. He won't let anything happen to them."

"Your grandpa is wonderful. Have you seen the looks exchanged between him and my aunt?"

Nick chuckled. "You'd have to be blind not to see that."

Sarah rotated toward him, looking up into his face. He was easy on the eyes, but what drew her was the man's integrity and compassion for others. Charlie had been a wonderful husband, and she missed him. She wanted what she'd had, but that meant she would have to take a risk, hoping she could find love that wouldn't be yanked away, especially after only a few years.

He placed a hand on each of her shoulders. "Cheering up Candy has been a success."

"Yes, but her pain will still have to be dealt with. Time will lessen it. I'm glad that Candy has Emma to talk to right now."

"And you. I've seen how much Candy listens to you. You're very important to her. Don't sell yourself short." He combed a stray strand of her hair behind her ear then slid his palm to cradle her jaw. "You're a beautiful woman inside and out."

A flush warmed her face. His nearness sent her blood racing through her body. In spite of her concerns of getting hurt, she wanted to kiss him. What would she have done if someone else had been the detective in charge of the murder case? Nick had thrown everything he had into solving the crime. She prayed that finding Jack

Coleman's body would lead to clues that would finally uncover who killed Mary and why.

She started to slide her arms around his neck and draw him to her. Before she could, he leaned toward her and kissed her as though he'd finally released all his passion. She felt cherished and desired, a warmth flowing through her. She hugged Nick, never wanting to let him go. Melting against him, she poured herself into the kiss, her embrace tightening around him.

"Anna and Candy, time to go inside," Bernie announced in a loud voice that penetrated the haze that clouded Sarah's mind.

Quickly, Nick and she parted, their gazes still bound as the girls and Bernie opened the back door. Sarah severed the visual bond and backed away from Nick, pulse racing through her body. She placed her palm against her hot cheek. He lived a dangerous life. What was she thinking? She had two children to take into consideration. Yet, she couldn't deny her developing feeling for Nick.

* * *

Monday morning, Sarah entered her office from her private entrance while Nick stood in the doorway, scanning the room. "Thanks for bringing me to work early." She walked to her mini refrigerator and put her lunch inside. "I've got so much to do with all that's been going on these past few weeks." She crossed to him. "I'll need to pick up Candy today at Emma's office. Will you be able to do that at four-thirty?"

"I should be, but if that changes, I'll have an officer escort you and Candy home from her appointment. I'll let you know."

"Call me if you get a breakthrough in the case."

"You'll be the first to know. I hope some piece of evidence from the car in the woods will give us a trail to follow. I've put a rush on processing the clues we've found in this case. The lab is backlogged, but I've called in a couple of favors to speed up the analysis."

Sarah sighed. "I hope you find what you need to break this case wide open. The kids need stability, especially Candy."

Nick's cell phone rang. "I've got to take this. Lock the door after I leave."

Sarah did then made her way to her desk, thinking of all she still needed to catch up with. First, she needed to listen to any message left on her office phone. She hadn't since Saturday because of all that had occurred yesterday. There was only one caller at two o'clock Sunday afternoon who left her with concerns.

"I've had it with my husband. He just doesn't understand what I'm going through. I tried to get him to identify with me. I'm leaving him."

When Sarah finished listening to Nancy Byrd, she tried to get in touch with her patient who had almost died in the grocery store bombing and had been struggling with what happened. The phone rang and rang. She left a message and hoped Nancy got back to her. She might still be sleeping since it was only eight in the morning. If Sarah had her car, she would be tempted to drive to Nancy's, but she didn't, and she had her first patient in an hour.

Could she get to Nancy's house and check on her then get back in time? She didn't live that far away, and there had been something in her patient's voice that bothered her. A sound of desperation?

She sat at her desk, trying to work, but she couldn't. Ten minutes later, she went out to see if Allie had come to work.

Thankfully, Allie walked into the outer office at the time she went to see if she had arrived. "Can I borrow your car? Nancy called me. I can't get hold of her, so I want to go to her house and make sure she's all right. I may be wrong, but I think she and her husband had a fight yesterday about what she's going through, and in her state, she can't deal with it."

Allie pulled her keys out of her pocket and handed them to Sarah. "What about your first appointment in forty minutes?"

"Ask Joe to wait, if possible. Nancy only lives ten minutes away from here. I hope I'm back before that. Also, look at the schedule and see where I can work Nancy in before her usual Thursday appointment."

"Okay. I'll text you with what I have."

"Good. Thank you for your car. I've got to get my life back to normal."

Allie chuckled. "Normal. What's that?"

"I'm not sure." Sarah hurried through her office, snatched up her purse, and headed out the private side door to the parking lot where Allie's car was.

Sarah made it to Nancy's place in nine minutes. The lights worked in her favor. As she walked up to the small cottage-type house with white paint and forest green shutters, Sarah realized she didn't know much about Nancy's husband. She rarely talked about him, so her call had taken Sarah by surprise. Why would one argument lead to leaving her husband? She pressed the doorbell twice. Her cell phone buzzed, and she looked at the screen. Her first patient would come back at the end of the day, so Sarah had time to talk with Nancy if she was here. When no one answered the door, she turned to leave.

Nancy opened the door. "I'm sorry it took me so long to respond."

Her patient appeared as though, while sleeping, she had wrestled with her sheet and had lost the battle. The bags under her eyes hinted that Nancy had been crying recently. "I got your message this morning and wanted to see if you were all right. May I come in? I have some time to talk now."

Nancy's gaze darted to the side, her hand gripping the door so tightly her knuckles were white. When her glance returned to Sarah, Nancy slowly stepped back.

Sarah moved forward. Her patient was close to falling apart. What happened this weekend?

"I'm sorry," Nancy whispered, her voice

quavering.

"Helping you when you need it is my job. You don't—"

"Shut the door now," a deep, raspy voice cut through the air.

Nancy scurried backwards while Sarah rotated to the right toward the sound of the voice. Her gaze connected with his bright blue one. A man, whose build fit what she'd seen on her security tape, held a gun on her.

THIRTEEN

"Tell me you have something," Nick said to Brad Thomas, his partner on Mary Phillips's case.

"Finally, we got lucky. I'm thankful the McVeys, who own the campground, put in a camera at the intersection of their dirt road and the highway. We have a picture of the man driving the Ford Fiesta. I'm running his photo through the system to see if an ID will come up. Also, the crime scene techs got a fingerprint from the car. Whether or not that proves to belong to our driver, I can't answer right now. We're trying to match the print."

"Did the camera show anyone leaving the dirt road after the Ford Fiesta went toward the campground? Someone had driven it to where Coleman's body was left, but where did that guy go after he dumped the car?"

"Good question." Brad took out his pad, looked at it, then said, "Nothing else was on the camera except the McVey family coming back to their campground about two hours later. I've asked for any video footage along that stretch of the main highway an hour before we saw the Ford going down the dirt road until you found the dead body yesterday. We should have it soon. I have an officer working on it." Again, he glanced at his notes. "While we're waiting for those searches to pan out, let's go visit Quinn Parker, who owns the car. Thankfully a license plate was found a few hundred yards from the vehicle when we increased our search perimeter this morning from where the car was parked. Then we were quickly able to match the Ford Fiesta to the plate."

"Did he call to report it stolen?" Nick headed for the exit, glad to be doing something while they waited for results.

"No."

The owner could be tied up in this case. "Do you have his photo?"

Brad held up the picture of his driver's license.

"He's a kid."

"Sixteen. I called his house and asked his mother to delay him from going to school until we arrive to talk to him."

Nick drove to the teenager's home on a street on the outskirts of Cimarron City. The Parker's place sat on an acre of land. As they approached the house, the front door swung open before he and Brad reached the porch. A woman in her late thirties, wearing a dress and heels, came outside, leaving her door opened only a few inches.

Nick showed Mrs. Parker his police badge. "We need to talk to Quinn about his car that we found not far from the lake."

"On the other side of town?"

"Yes. It was in the woods. We're still processing it."

"When did you find it?"

"Yesterday."

"Why's it taking so long? My son needs it for school then his job after school."

"It's tied up in a murder case."

She blanched when she heard the last two words. "Do I need to call an attorney? Quinn is a good student and a hard worker. He just discovered this morning it was missing when he went out to the shed where he kept it."

"You can call an attorney, and you can sit in on our interview if you want. It's important we talk to him as soon as possible."

She checked her watch. "I need to be at work in half an hour." She swung the door open wide and gestured for them to go inside.

Quinn stood in the entrance into the living room off the foyer. The first things Nick noticed were the teen's pale face and his eyes cast downward, as though there was something extremely interesting on the tile floor.

"Quinn, I'm Detective Nick Davidson, and this is my partner, Brad Thomas. We need to talk to you about your stolen car."

The teenager looked at Nick. "I don't know anything. I went out this morning, and it was gone. Now I'm gonna be late for school." The kid snapped his mouth closed as if that was the end of the conversation.

"Why didn't you call it in this morning when you found it gone?"

His gaze dropped back to the floor. "I—I was trying to—figure out how I was going to get to school."

"Who took the car, Quinn? The person had a key. It was left at the crime scene."

"Crime scene!" The boy's wide brown eyes dominated his facial features.

"Do I need to take you down to headquarters?" Nick asked while Quinn began breathing fast but not seeming to draw much air into his lungs.

"Chris Holmes. He's my best friend. He needed a car for a date on Friday. My mom won't let me loan it out. I keep a spare key in a box behind my front left tire. Chris is the only one who knows that and the only person I would let drive it."

"Quinn!" Mrs. Parker came forward and closed the space between her and her son. "Why didn't you know it was gone yesterday?"

"Because Chris called me and wanted to keep it for Saturday night too. I thought he brought it back to the shed. I didn't need it 'til this morning."

Mrs. Parker set her hands on her waist. "If you ever get to drive your car again, and that is in doubt at the moment, you'll park it next to the garage instead of in the shed out back, and there will be no spare keys kept in the car but in my purse."

"Where does Chris live?"

Quinn gave Nick the address. "He'll be at school right now."

"If you think of anything else, please call." Nick handed the teen his card. "We may have more questions in the future. Don't text Chris and warn him we're coming to see him."

"Yes, sir. I won't."

Nick said good-bye to Mrs. Parker and left the house with Brad. "What do you think?"

"He'll notify his friend, but I've been wrong in the past."

"I believe the car was stolen from Chris, and he's trying to cover it up with Quinn."

"Let's go by headquarters and check out what we can about Chris Parker before we interview him. It's on the way to the high school."

As Nick approached the police station, he got a call on his cell phone. He looked at the name and quickly pressed his button.

"Allie, is something wrong?"

"I've called Sarah twice, and she hasn't answered either time. She should have been back thirty minutes ago."

Nick pulled into the parking lot at headquarters. "Where did she go?"

"To see a client, Nancy Byrd, at her house. She borrowed my car."

His gut tightened. "Do you know why?"

"Nancy left a message for her. I gather she had a hard time over the weekend."

"What's the address? Does anyone else live at Nancy's house?"

"The address is 3915 Pine Street. Nancy has a husband who lives there. That's all I know."

"Thanks." He disconnected the call. Chills flashed down his spine. "Why would Sarah leave her office to speak to a client when all this is going on around her?"

"What's going on?" Brad asked.

"Sarah's not picking up her phone after making a home visit to a client, and her secretary says she should have returned by now. I don't know why this woman comes to see her." Nick ran a hand through his hair.

"There's only one way to find out." Brad nodded.

Nick pulled out of the parking lot heading for the address Allie had given him.

Ten minutes later, Nick pulled to a stop several houses away from Nancy's. First, he tried to get a hold of Sarah on her cell phone. When she didn't answer, Nick got out of the car and looked at Brad over the top of his vehicle. "I don't have a good feeling about this."

Nick started for the house. As he

mounted the steps to the porch, a scream resonated through the air.

* * *

Nancy's husband was Sarah's stalker. Why? She'd never met him, and what she and Nancy had talked about in her sessions had been about surviving a near-death situation. She'd been at IFI as a part-time employee when the building had to be evacuated, only to be hurt in the bombing at the grocery store later that week.

Sarah sat in the chair Mark Byrd indicated while he gripped his wife's upper arm so tightly that he would leave bruises. Silent tears ran down Nancy's cheeks.

Finally, he shoved his wife onto the couch. "I told you no more sessions. I don't want you telling her," he waved his gun at Sarah, "our secrets. It's no one else's business."

Gripping the arms of the chair, she drew in one deep breath after another to calm the fear rising inside her. She had to remain calm. "She didn't tell me any of your secrets. Our sessions were about dealing with being a survivor of the bombing. That's all."

"Liar. You'd say whatever you need to. I've been to a person like you. I know your tricks."

This time he pointed the weapon right at Sarah. She wanted to make him see she wasn't a liar, but the man was worked up and was ready to explode any second. Her mouth went dry while her pulse rate shot up.

Nancy's husband stepped toward her. "See, you can't even deny it."

"No, Mark. She isn't lying. That was all I talked about," Nancy said.

He spun around and charged his wife, raising his arm and striking Nancy across her face so quickly that Sarah couldn't stop him.

Nancy's loud scream pealed through the room.

* * *

Nick ran toward the home, bounded up the steps, and tried the door. Locked. The shriek came from the right. He moved that way, peered into a window, and quickly assessed the situation. Sarah sat in a chair while another woman lay on the couch, her face bleeding from a cut. A man held a gun, waving it around. His wild gestures and angry expression indicated a person falling apart.

Brad mounted the stairs to the porch and whispered, "I've called this in."

Nick hurried back to the door and pulled out his tools to pick the lock quietly. If he tried to kick the door down, the assailant could possibly shoot Sarah and Nancy then flee out the back. "I'm going in." *If this works.* "Go to the rear door and try to get inside that way. At least, be there if the guy runs out back. I'm leaving my cell phone on so you can hear what's going on," he whispered to his partner.

Brad left, and within two minutes, Nick picked the lock, withdrew his gun, and slowly opened the door, making sure he was as quiet as possible. He kept his attention trained on the entrance into the living room. His heartbeat thudded as he crept forward, adrenaline pumping through his body, giving him a surge of energy.

"Mark, other than your name and that you're Nancy's husband, I don't know anything about you." Sarah spoke in a calm, even-toned voice as though she'd studied destressing techniques in a volatile situation.

Nick flattened himself against the wall on the right side of the entrance and glimpsed

Mark Byrd.

He faced Sarah, combing his hair repeatedly while waving the gun around, its barrel thankfully still pointed toward the floor. Nick caught a brief glimpse of Mark's vivid blue eyes, like the picture of the man caught on Nick's camera. The assailant's gaze widened with rage.

"Liar! I saw my name in Nancy's file."

"From my office?" Sarah's glance brushed Nick, but she continued her scan of her surroundings as though she hadn't seen him. It had been no longer than a second before she'd moved on to Nancy.

"Yes. I have a *right* to see what was said about me!" Mark yelled and lifted his gun halfway up.

Nick sneaked toward Mark while keeping his weapon pointed at the man. "Drop your gun. Now! I can shoot you before you pull the trigger."

Mark glanced over his shoulder, his eyes wider, his look wild.

"Don't think about it." Nick moved a step closer, seeing a man debating whether to shoot or not.

"Please, Mark. You need help," Nancy said.

The guy stood, his look drilling into Nick

as though Mark were trying to read his mind. Nick narrowed his eyes. "Don't make me shoot you. Put your weapon on the floor. Now."

A few long seconds passed before the woman's husband squatted and placed the revolver on the floor.

Nick spied Brad coming into the living room from the back. While Nick kept his weapon on Mark, Brad came forward, snatched up the gun, and put handcuffs on the assailant.

The second the guy was secured, Sarah rose and rushed to Nancy's side. "Are you all right?" She examined the cut on her patient's cheek. "Let's go into the bathroom and take care of this." Sarah looked toward Nick. "Okay?"

"Yeah. Backup is arriving." Nick let Sarah and Nancy leave the room before they took Mark Byrd outside to be transported to the police station.

As Nick escorted the assailant to a patrol car, he asked, "Did you send flowers to Dr. Collins?"

Mark nodded.

"Why?"

"To make her life miserable like mine. There's nothing in the law that forbids sending flowers to another person."

The man had calmed down, and the smile he gave Nick sent goosebumps down his arms.

"But there is for assault and holding a person hostage," Nick said as he turned the attacker over to a patrol officer.

Once Mark Byrd was secured in the back of the police car, Nick holstered his gun and curled his hands into tight balls. Memories of the time he'd almost died being caught up in a domestic dispute that had left one person dead and another injured, not including him being shot, deluged him with an onslaught of feelings from fear to anger he tried to keep locked up. Slowly he opened his fists as if releasing his intense emotions, inhaled several deep breaths, and started back toward the house to make sure Sarah and Nancy were all right.

* * *

Sarah finished carefully cleaning Nancy's face and putting a bandage over it to stop the bleeding. "You should see a doctor in case you need stitches."

"I'll call my doctor."

"Has your husband hit you before

today?"

"Yes, yesterday for the first time."

"Why?"

"Because in his home office, I found photographs he'd taken of your file on me. I immediately called you, but shortly after that, he caught me with the folder. He took it away and knocked the breath out of me. He wouldn't let me go anywhere or call anyone. He spent the rest of the day ranting at me. I knew he was having issues at work, and lately, he'd become angry at the slightest thing, but he wouldn't get help. He kept telling me he was all right. I was the one who was seeing a counselor."

"Did he admit to trashing my office?" Sarah wanted at least to have closure with the bouquets and the break-in.

When Nancy nodded, a cloak of relief fell over Sarah until she remembered there was a bigger threat hanging over her head. What had Candy seen at her home? Was Candy safe now that her father had been murdered, or was there something else going on that they didn't know anything about? After all, Sarah doubted that Jack Coleman's body being left in a car near Nick's property was a coincidence. "He's here." Candy had said.

Sarah didn't think they had dealt with the man who Candy had seen at school a few days ago. Where was this guy, especially now that Jack Coleman was dead? Who killed Candy's father, and why?

FOURTEEN

Sarah slanted a look at Nick as he drove her to the ranch. "Are you all right?"

"Shouldn't I be asking you that question?"

"I'm okay. I'm concerned about you. Essentially what happened this morning was a domestic dispute. I just wanted to make sure you were all right after what occurred at Nancy's."

His facial expression tensed, his grip on the steering wheel tightening, his knuckles white. "I'm working through it. When I decided to continue being a police officer, I came to terms that my job can be dangerous and risky. I've turned to the Lord to watch over me. Someone has to fight to make this world safe for others. This morning I didn't think about the previous domestic dispute five years ago. I did what needed to be done then processed the whole situation afterward. With time and God's help, I've learned to manage my emotions. I'm not going to let that original shooter drive me away from what I've always wanted to do." Nick pulled into the driveway to his house.

"Good. If you ever need someone to listen to you, I'm here for you."

He let his hold on the steering wheel go and clasped her hand. "Thank you. I appreciate your support. The same goes for me. This morning was tough on everyone."

His soft gaze taking her in with concern brought to the surface all the feelings she was experiencing in his presence. She was falling in love and wasn't sure how to deal with it. She swallowed hard, smiled at him, and opened the door. "I know you need to return to work. It sounds like you're getting closer to finding out what's going on with Jack Coleman's murder."

"One fingerprint from the Fiesta I found in the woods came back belonging to Larry Moore, who went to prison for robbing a jewelry store in Houston. He was recently paroled."

"How is Jack Coleman connected to Larry Moore? Mary never said anything about her husband being in jail before his conviction about the abuse."

"I don't know. I received a text from Brad right before I drove you here, but I'm returning to headquarters to see what I can find. Moore got a little reckless, thankfully. This is the biggest clue we've gotten so far. The car was wiped down, but he missed one, which has led to identifying him."

Sarah smiled. "Good. Hopefully, everything will settle down, and my life will get back to normal."

"Rest. I'll let you know tonight what I've learned." He put his hand on the lever to open the door.

"I've got this. Stay in the car." She quickly exited his SUV.

Emotionally drained after the early morning confrontation with Mark Byrd, she mounted the steps to the porch at Nick's house, trying to pretend everything was all right while he sat in the car and waited until she went inside before he left. All Sarah wanted to do was take a nap. The girls would be home from school in a couple of hours. Maybe she could sleep for a while.

Before she went into the house, Aunt

Louise swung the front door open and gave her a hug. "I'm so glad you found your stalker and that you're okay." Her aunt started toward the kitchen. "I can fix you something to eat."

Sarah followed her. Although she was hungry, exhaustion overrode everything else. "I'm going to lie down for a while. I feel drained. I had to cancel my patients and work them into my schedule later this week. I stayed with Nancy and tried to help her through the ordeal with her husband's meltdown. The signs were there, but Nancy didn't see them because she was dealing with her own trauma."

"I think a nap will do you good. I'll take care of the girls when they get home from school. Don't worry about them." Aunt Louise waved her hand toward the exit. "Go."

Sarah smiled. "Thanks. I thank God every day that you came into my life after Charlie died."

"I thank God you and your daughters are part of my life. Now go." Again, she waved her toward the hallway.

Sarah trudged toward the bedroom she shared with her aunt, closed the door, and flopped down onto the bed. Her purse slipped from her hand and fell to the floor in front of the nightstand. She didn't have the energy to pick it up. Her eyelids slid closed, and sleep blanketed her...

Sarah's eyes bolted open, and she glanced at her watch. She had slept for over two hours. She hadn't wanted to sleep that long. She'd wanted to check on Nancy and then see the girls.

An eerie quiet shrouded her. She shot up straight in bed. Although the air wasn't chilly, she shivered. She swung her legs to the left and sat up. Her mind still groggy from a deep sleep, she rose slowly, chuckling at seeing her flats still on her feet. She realized how tired she'd been earlier, but not enough to take off her shoes while she slept. It underscored how exhausted she had really been.

She started for the hallway to see what Anna and Candy were doing. It was too quiet. They must have gone to the barn. She gripped the doorknob and turned it.

A crashing sound nearby resonated through the air. She went into the short corridor and headed for the girls' bedroom right next to hers.

"We've got to hurry. Where is it? We've got to find it now and get out of town," a man with a deep voice said—a voice she hadn't heard before.

Another unknown man swore. "We've got to check the whole house. Go into the room next to this while I finish in here. We don't have a lot of time. It has to be here somewhere. If not, it's with her."

What were they trying to find? Their desperation resonated through their tone.

Sarah whirled around and hurried back into her room, quietly shutting the door when she wanted to slam it and lock it—if there was a lock. There wasn't one. Instead, she quickly jammed herself under the bed and prayed the intruder didn't look there. As the doorknob turned, she reached for her purse on the floor and snatched it toward her. Her pulse rate shot up. Its quick pulsating clanged against her skull.

A guy wearing wingtips walked around the bedroom, opening and closing drawers and the closet. He tossed a few items onto the floor. Then ten minutes later, he left.

She delved into her purse and pulled out her cell phone. He'd left the door opened, so she needed to be vigilant and quiet, but she texted Nick, "At least two intruders in your house. Warn everyone to stay away" and hoped he saw it immediately. Then she silenced the ringer, so a call wouldn't alert the intruders to her location.

She heard more of what the guys were doing while going from one room to another. What were they looking for? Was their first room to search the girls'? But mostly, she wanted to know where Aunt Louise, Anna, Candy, and Bernie were.

* * *

Nick and Brad walked into the Cimarron City Auto Park and found Chris Holmes at the counter. Brad approached the teenager head-on while Nick came from the side where the kid would flee if he chose to try and escape.

"Tell us about the Ford Fiesta you borrowed last weekend," Nick said.

Chris froze, his eyes round. "I didn't do anything wrong. Someone stole it sometime Friday night after I came home."

"When was that?" Brad asked, tapping his police badge that hung around his neck.

The teen looked down at the floor. "After two, but I didn't realize it until Saturday afternoon when I was gonna take it back to Quinn."

"Why didn't you report it stolen or at the

least tell Quinn?"

"Scared." The seventeen-year-old's words were hard to discern due to his mumbling.

Nick joined Brad. "Why were you scared? Quinn told me you're best friends. You had no control over someone stealing the car. Did you think whoever stole it was going to bring it back?"

Chris shrugged. "I was hoping it was some kids joyriding, and they'd bring it back before I had to return it to Quinn. Where was it found? Is it okay?"

"It's in one piece and will be returned to Quinn when we're through with it. A dead body was discovered in the trunk. Are you sure you didn't see anything? Do you normally come home at two in the morning?"

Nick carefully watched the boy's facial expression as he let him know about the murder victim. The teenager's right eye kept twitching, and he stiffened at the mention of the corpse. "You're hiding something. Do you know who took the car?"

Chris opened and closed his mouth as though he was lost for words.

"Promise me you won't tell my parents where I was."

Nick shook his head. "I can't do that, but I can take you down to headquarters right now."

The kid's shoulders sagged forward, and he released a long sigh. "I parked it at O'Leary's Bar, and when I came outside, it was gone."

"You didn't have a date like you told Quinn?"

He nodded. "I met some college friends inside. They were home for the weekend."

Nick held out his hand. "Give me your false ID."

Chris shuffled his feet and stared at the floor.

"If you do, I'll let you go with a warning this time. If you don't, I'll take you to jail."

Grumbling, Chris dug his billfold out of his back pocket, removed his fake driver's license, and gave it to Nick.

"Now the others."

"Others?"

Nick's cell phone buzzed, and he withdrew it from his pocket to see if it was something he needed to deal with right away. He saw the message from Sarah, and it felt like his heart plummeted into his stomach. "You've exhausted my patience. Detective Thomas will finish with you." Then

Nick pulled Brad away and whispered, "There are a couple of men in my house. Sarah's hiding from them. I don't know anything else. I'll call for backup."

"I'll be right behind you."

Nick ran from the store and hopped into his car. After placing a call to the police station and reporting what was happening at the ranch, he floored his accelerator.

He pictured the ones who would be home at this time: Sarah, Anna, Candy, Louise and Grandpa. Each one was very important to him. This had to end now.

He called his grandpa. "There are two men in the house. Where are you?"

"The barn. Louise and the kids are with me. I can go—"

"No! Stay there and hide everyone in case the intruders come to the barn."

"Don't worry. I will."

Nick disconnected the call and focused on getting to the ranch before someone was killed.

Please, God, let me arrive in time before anyone is hurt.

* * *

Sweat dripped off Sarah's face onto the

hardwood floor under the bed. She had no idea if Nick received her message. She stiffened at the sound of footsteps approaching the room again. Earlier she heard one of the intruders say they had to find it now. Find what? Whatever they sought was connected to Candy, and the longer the guys searched, the more frantic they became.

A text from Nick that popped up on her cell phone screen read, "On my way."

She exhaled then drew in a deep breath. The man wearing wingtips returned to the bedroom where she was. She stuffed her phone into the depths of her purse. Again, he pulled open the drawers, but this time its contents were tossed on the floor. Across the room where the huge intruder stood, she watched him turn the drawer over to check and see if something was taped to it.

He swung around as she scooted deeper under the king-size bed. Suddenly he charged toward her refuge, stooped, and tried to grip her leg.

"I need help in here," the assailant yelled, no doubt to his partner.

The second man scurried through the doorway. "What's going on? We don't have time for this."

"Dr. Collins is under the bed."

They knew who she was.

"I need your help to get her."

The new guy squatted on the other side, pulled out his weapon with a silencer on it, and leaned down. "I'll shoot you if you don't come out." He paused a couple of seconds and added, "Now!"

She didn't have a choice. At least she was able to get a message to Nick. She prayed he arrived soon. Leaving her handbag on the floor, she dragged herself toward the intruder holding the gun on her. When he got a hold on her, he clamped her arm and jerked her out from under the bed.

His grip dug into her skin while he set his gun on the dresser behind him. "Where's the girl's Teddy bear?"

"I don't know. I came home and took a nap. I just woke up and found you two were here."

"Not the right answer." He punched her in the stomach.

The force of his fist striking her knocked the breath from her, and the strength from the blow drained the force that held her upright. She gasped for air.

"Again, where is the girl?"

She had to stall until the police arrived.

Although knowing he had to be talking about Candy, Sarah braced herself for another punch. "Why do you want a Teddy bear?"

This time the power behind the hit sent her flying backward onto the bed. Pain shot through her body, her lungs burning from lack of air.

Wingtip glanced out the window. "Boss, I see a child running after a dog outside the barn."

No!

The one in charge gripped her arm and dragged her up against him. He stuck his face in hers and said, "You're coming with us."

The stench of his garlic-laced breath nauseated Sarah. He clasped her against his broad chest and pointed his revolver at her. "One wrong move and I'll shoot you. Now walk. We're going to the barn."

* * *

Nick parked along the paved road behind his ranch with other police officers arriving and following suit. He took out his binoculars and assessed the situation at his house and barn. Her text said two intruders were inside his home. Where was everyone? Did

Grandpa manage to hide the girls and Louise? At this point, he needed to focus most of the officers on his house since that was where the assailants were—at least he prayed they were still there and not at the barn. He was hoping that his grandfather had his rifle with him. He had carried it with him since Sarah and her family had come to Nick's place to stay. They usually went to the barn after school. So, was Sarah safely hiding in his home?

The police officers squatted behind Nick's car. "Brad, take two officers to the barn," Nick ordered. "Make sure the girls, my grandpa, and Louise are there and safe. Leave the officers with them, and you come to the house. The rest of us will enter my place. I'm going to assume that's where the intruders are. They were fifteen minutes ago." Nick slowly rose and withdrew his weapon. "We'll use the cover of the trees as much as possible.

As he crept forward, he wished there wasn't a thirty-yard stretch of lawn with little cover for protection. Where was Bella? If an unknown person was on the ranch, she would be barking, a lot. It was too quiet.

At the edge of the trees, Nick came to a halt, putting his arm up. Candy ran out of the rear of the barn, chasing Trixie. She scooped her up into her arms and went back inside. Relief flitted through him. The girls were at the barn, and obviously, the two crooks weren't. He prayed the intruders didn't see Candy grabbing her puppy.

Nick signaled for two officers to head for the front of his house. He waited to move until one went to the left side while the other moved to the right. Then Nick waved to Brad and the two officers, assigned to secure the barn, to go there. He motioned to Officer Brown and Nelson for them to make their way to the rear entrance with him. But before they took one step, the door opened.

Nick locked gazes with the thug, Larry Moore, who had Sarah plastered against his chest, his weapon pointed at her head.

FIFTEEN

Sweat drenched Sarah. The feel of the gun barrel pressed against her head sparked a bolt of panic that zipped down her body. She might not get out of this alive. She slid her gaze to the other intruder slightly ahead of her and to the left. He raised his weapon and pointed it toward Nick. She swung her attention to him. His revolver was aimed at the brute who held her.

Lord, help me. Nick.

"Drop your weapons. You won't escape." Nick shouted loud enough that she hoped Aunt Louise and Bernie heard him and stayed in the barn with the girls and the two officers to protect them. Brad was already making his way to the house.

"I'll release her when I get away from here. Move back or else I'll shoot her."

Nick kept his laser-focused attention on her captor. "If you do, you're a dead man. I'm an expert shot. You're surrounded by the police with more to come."

Her captor started moving backward toward the door into the house.

All the strength drained from Sarah. Her legs gave out, and she slid downward.

* * *

The second Sarah's body began sinking toward the ground, exposing more of the man's chest, the weapon was no longer pointed at Sarah's head. Nick aimed his gun at the assailant's right shoulder and pulled the trigger. Freed, Sarah stumbled toward a nearby chair on the patio and collapsed onto it.

The bullet hit Sarah's abductor right where Nick intended, throwing the man off balance and causing him to drop his weapon. Surprised, he clutched his wound as he staggered back. Nick rushed the guy while Brad and another police officer ran toward the second intruder with their pistols pointed at him. He surrendered, laying his weapon on the ground.

Nick focused totally on the assailant who reached toward his weapon that lay on the patio. Nick made it to the firearm before the injured man and kicked it away. The other officers from the front of the house rounded the corner and headed toward him.

Nick swung his attention to Sarah, her arms crossed over her chest. "Okay, Sarah?"

"Yes." The word came out in a shaky voice, sweat running down her face.

"Call for an ambulance and take care of the downed guy." As his team followed his orders, he moved quickly to Sarah. "Did he hurt you?"

"I'll be okay. Check to make sure the girls are in the barn."

"They're safe with Grandpa and Louise. I have two officers there too."

"Good." Sarah tried to push herself to her feet, but halfway through the task, she crumpled back onto the cushioned chair, wincing.

"You need to take it easy. If you want, I'll call my grandpa and have him put Anna and Candy on the phone."

She shook her head. "I need to gather myself first before I see them, but please call him to make sure everything's okay there. I'll feel better."

He took out his cell phone and connected with his grandpa. "Are the girls all right?"

"Yes. When a gunshot sounded, I told them it was probably a car backfiring. I didn't want them worrying. I've got them helping me feed the animals. They didn't see the police come to the barn. They were in a stable brushing a horse. The officers are guarding the front and back entrances."

"I'll tell Sarah. We'll come and get you all when the house has been cleared of the two assailants." He disconnected his call and looked toward her. Her pale coloring and pain-filled eyes made him pause. "Are you all right? Did he hurt you?"

Her eyelids slid closed for a few seconds.

He squatted down in front of her. "Sarah, what happened?"

"He hit me in the stomach a couple of times."

Nick squeezed his hands into a tight ball. The urge to pounce on the guy and beat him up swamped Nick. He started to rise.

She placed her hand on his shoulder. "Don't. Just get me to the ER. It's probably best to be checked by a doctor."

This time Nick stood and turned to assess the situation. "Be right back." He walked to Brad, who had handcuffed the second intruder and had him on his feet. Nick motioned for an officer to come and take care of the man. "Take him to the station."

When they left, Nick turned to Brad. "I need you to wrap this up. An ambulance is coming for him." Nick gestured toward the guy who hurt Sarah. "He hit Sarah in the stomach a few times. She doesn't look well. I'm driving her to the hospital. I can get her there faster than waiting for another ambulance."

"Don't worry. I'll take care of this."

"Let my grandpa know what's happening and where I am. When I know something concrete, I'll call them about Sarah's status."

Nick hurried to her and helped her to stand. "If for any reason you can't make it, let me know. Are your keys on the hook in the kitchen?"

"Yes."

"Good. Taking your car is faster than me driving around to pick you up." He gestured toward his SUV parked on the paved road two hundred yards away with a fence he would have to get her over. "Less walking for you too."

She tried to smile, but it didn't last.

"Thanks."

He cuddled her next to him, and together they mounted the one step into the house. He headed for the kitchen, snagged the keys to her vehicle, and went into the garage. As he backed out and drove toward the highway, he slanted a look at her.

Her gaze connected with his. "They were looking for Candy's Teddy bear."

"Why?"

"They were looking for something. Don't know what." Her body tensed. She'd slumped against the window, her eyes closed.

"Are you okay?" he asked as he turned onto the road into town.

"No," came out in a weak voice.

Nick sped as fast as he could. A block away, Sarah clutched her stomach and leaned over, throwing up onto the floor mat.

He called to have a gurney and staff waiting for her at the ER doors.

When he reached the hospital, a nurse and orderly were there and assisted her onto the gurney while Nick rounded the back of her car. He followed them inside. The next half an hour crawled by while he waited for the doctor to tell him what was wrong with Sarah.

When Dr. Richard came to the waiting room, Nick stood and met him halfway. "What's wrong?"

"Her appendix has ruptured. I'm taking her into emergency surgery to remove it. She wanted you to call her aunt and let her know what's going on."

"I will. How bad is it?"

"Bad enough that I need to do the surgery right away. The man who punched her hit her so hard it moved her appendix and it burst."

When she was wheeled toward surgery, she was as pale as the white sheets she lay on. The sight made him more determined to make sure both men never left prison. He hurried toward her and said, "I'll let Louise know. I'll be here for you."

Her dull eyes stared at him as though she didn't really hear him. He squeezed her hand right before she vanished from view behind the double doors to the surgery rooms. He felt a part of him was going with her—his heart. If anything happened to her, he didn't know what he would do.

For an hour, he prowled the waiting room for family and friends of surgery patients until he had to get away. Do something to help Sarah. He found the chapel not far from the waiting room and stepped inside. He sat in the front pew and bowed his head. The quiet enveloped him, and all the feelings he had tried to hold back swamped him.

"Father, please let Sarah make it through the surgery. She has people who love and care for her. The girls will need her. I need her."

When that last sentence came from his mouth, in that moment, he realized he was falling in love with Sarah.

* * *

Four days later, Nick turned off the highway into his ranch. He slowed the car and shifted his glance to Sarah. "Okay?"

"Yes, but I'll feel better when you can tell me there are no more threats to me and my family."

"It should take only a couple of more days to track down all leads and make sure there aren't other people coming after you or anyone else involved in this case."

"And the million dollars' worth of diamonds are back to their rightful owner?"

"Yes, and Louise was successfully able to sew up Candy's big Teddy bear as if no one had ever opened it up."

"I wish I could have been there for Candy."

After parking his car in front of the house, Nick clasped her hand. "She didn't even know. Louise did it while she was at school. If Candy noticed something was off, she hasn't said anything about it."

When Sarah tried to turn toward him, she winced. "I've never had surgery before. I'm having a hard time keeping myself restrained because I have a three-inch scar where they took my appendix out."

"I'll remind you to take it easy. I'm just glad I got you to the hospital. When your appendix burst, you needed to get into surgery right away because of the infection that could spread."

Sarah sighed. "That day could have ended so badly. In one sense, that guy, Larry Moore, who punched me in the stomach, did me a favor. I don't know if I would ever have thought or had the courage to slide down his body, allowing you to shoot him in the shoulder. My legs just gave out."

"God working in mysterious ways?"

"I think so. You never told me how Larry Moore was connected to Mary's ex-husband."

"That's one of the loose ends we finally solved earlier today. Coleman was in on the robbery of the diamonds five years ago with Moore, the guy who left a fingerprint in the Ford Fiesta, and Earl Clinton. Coleman was the getaway man. They were supposed to meet up and share the loot, but Moore and Clinton were captured and sent to prison for the robbery. They got out of jail four months ago. They were supposed to meet Coleman, but it didn't happen because he'd ended up in jail for abusing Mary and Candy. He wouldn't tell Moore or Clinton where the diamonds were until he was released from prison. Coleman had kept their share as they agreed because Clinton scared Coleman. He'd known both of them for years. He'd put the diamonds in the Teddy bear and gave it to his daughter for safekeeping. When he'd served his time for the abuse conviction, he hadn't counted on Mary moving to Cimarron City and hiding from him. The three of them searched for where Mary moved. Clinton found out, and they all came here to get the stuffed animal."

"Did you ever find the black pickup that was seen on the street behind Mary's house as the possible getaway vehicle after Mary's death?"

"Yes, parked about a quarter of a mile off the paved road behind my ranch the day the two broke into my home. Their fingerprints were all over the pickup. Also, we found in the truck a butcher knife with Mary's blood on it, but there were no fingerprints on it. The knife was wiped clean except for a speck of blood by the handle."

Sarah frowned, her eyebrows slashing downward. "Did they tell you how they knew where Candy was staying?"

Nick nodded. "They staked out the school and followed her here, most likely the day that Candy hid from us."

Sarah didn't speak for a long moment. When she did, it came with a tightness in her voice. "I should have realized. Children don't make things up. They react to the stimuli around them. She'd seen her mother's killer the day of the murder and when they were near the house. But which one killed Mary?"

"According to Clinton, he said Coleman did because he had a score to settle with her. Moore backed him up, although he didn't sound one hundred percent convincing. Who better to blame a murder on than the man you killed? With all the crimes they committed, they'll be in jail for a long time. I think on the day of Mary's murder one was in the truck waiting for them to flee the crime scene. I don't believe there were three of them in Mary's house. I'd like to think that even Jack Coleman had some decency in him. Maybe he threatened to turn on them after they killed Mary and were going after Candy."

"I got the impression from Candy that it wasn't Jack who attacked Mary. That brings me a little comfort. When she's older, she may seek answers to what actually happened. I'll truly be able to tell her that the police couldn't prove that her father was her mother's killer, and he may have died trying to protect her."

"Oh, by the way, we finally got the DNA test back on the gum found by your car when it was vandalized. It was Mark Byrd's. We didn't need it to tie him to being your stalker. He admitted it. He's getting treatment, but he'll go before a judge for what he did."

"All I want is for him to get the help he needs."

"He will." Nick squeezed her hand. "We need to go inside. I see the girls peeking out the window."

She chuckled, the sound music to his

ears. "I'm surprised they lasted this long."

When she started to open the door, he said, "Wait right there," then hopped out of the car and rounded the front to help Sarah out of the SUV. He offered her his hand and assisted her from the vehicle.

As he walked with her to the porch, he thought about the showdown several days ago at his house. He could have lost Sarah, and until the moment he saw Moore holding a gun to her head, he hadn't realized how much he cared about her.

No, more than cared. He loved her. But with all the trauma surrounding the past week, how could he tell if it was the kind of love that would last a lifetime?

Candy and Anna disappeared from the large picture window in his living room. The front door swung open, and the two girls raced down the steps toward them. Louise came outside with his grandpa.

"Girls, remember what I told you," Sarah's aunt said in a stern voice.

Candy slowed first, quickly followed by Anna.

"Remember what I told you about hugging her." Louise stayed on the porch with Grandpa next to her.

Anna latched onto her mother's right arm

while Candy did the same with the left one.

Her daughter looked up at Sarah. "I missed you this much." She let go of Sarah and stretched her arms wide open.

Sarah laughed. "That's how much I love you both. Let's go inside. I need to sit down."

The two girls strolled with Sarah into Nick's house.

In that moment, he longed for a wife and children. For years, he'd let his job define his life, but he wanted more. He'd gotten a taste of what it would be like. He was the last into his home. In the middle of everyone was Bella who had recovered nicely after the two thugs had tainted her outside water bowl with a knockout drug and tied her up in the forest, so she wouldn't alert anyone something was wrong that day when her haven had been invaded.

* * *

Tired, but at peace. Finally. Sarah leaned back against the sofa cushion with Bella on one side of her and Nick on the other. Candy and Anna were getting ready for bed and would return to say good night after they had their baths.

"It was a fun evening, especially when the girls rode 'their' horse up to the patio." Sarah stroked Bella and was so glad that she hadn't died from being poisoned.

"They're getting good at riding. At first, I wasn't sure Candy would get on Sadie, but now her smile is so big when she's riding. Anna asked me if she could sleep in the stall where her mare is kept. I had to nix that idea."

"Thank you. It sounds like you've been spending time with them while I've been in the hospital."

"They're special. I'm going to hate to see them leave here. Your family has brought some life to this ranch."

Looking into his beautiful gray eyes melted her heart. In their depths, she could forget what had happened recently. She cupped his face. "You saved my life. How can I thank you?"

"You already have, but," he leaned toward her, placing his hands over hers, "I can think of one way."

When he kissed her, she closed her eyes, and it felt as though she had soared high above the ground. All the feelings she had suppressed since Charlie had died flowed through her body.

He pulled back a few inches. "I love you, Sarah. I want to build on this relationship. When I saw that gun at your head, all my dreams for a happy future withered. Life is too short. I want to spend what's left of mine with you."

"So do I." She'd had enough time in the hospital to decide what her feelings were toward Nick. And each time she'd considered what she was feeling, she knew it was love. When he wasn't working on the case or making sure the girls were all right, he was beside her hospital bed, supporting her and being there as she recovered from the surgery. "I love you too." This time she instigated the kiss and wound her arms around him.

She only broke away when she heard giggles coming from the entrance into the den. When she looked at Anna and Candy, she smiled. "Are you all ready for bed?"

Grinning, they both nodded.

Nick rose and presented his hand. She fitted hers within it, and he assisted her up while Bella hopped down from the sofa and trotted toward the girls. He leaned toward her ear and whispered, "I could get used to this every night."

"Me, too."

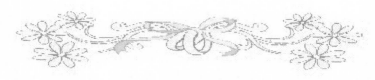

Together with their family

Sarah Collins
&
Nick Davidson

Sarah and Nick invite you to share
in their joy
as they exchange marriage vows
on Friday, the Fourteen of February
Two Thousand and Twenty
at Seven O'clock in the Evening.

The Church of Hope
5835 Buffalo Street
Cimarron City, OK

Dear Readers,

This was a tough book to write with a lot of twists and turns. But this story is a special one to me because of the dog, Bella. There is a real Bella that is part corgi and bull terrier. She is loving and a great pet for a family with children. My two granddaughters picked her out at the shelter, and it was the best decision. The photo of the dog on the cover is from my granddaughter who took many pictures of her dog until I found one that would work on the cover. Getting a dog to sit still can be hard work. Well worth it for me.

Best wishes,
Margaret Daley

Books in the
EVERYDAY HEROES
Series

HUNTED, Book One
Murder. On the Run. Second Chances.

Luke Michaels' relaxing camping trip ends when he witnesses a woman being thrown from a bridge. He dives into the river to save her, shocked to find her wrapped in chains. As a canine search and rescue volunteer, Luke has assisted many victims, but never a beauty whose defeated gaze ignites his primal urge to protect. When Megan Witherspoon's killers make it clear they won't stop, Luke fights to save her, but can he keep her alive long enough to find out who is after her?

OBSESSED, Book Two
Stalker. Arson. Murder.

When a stalker ruthlessly targets people she loves, a woman flees her old life, creating a new identity as Serena Remington. Her plan to escape the madman and lead him away from family and friends worked for three years. Now he's back. With nowhere else to run, her only choice is war. Quinn Taylor, her neighbor and a firefighter with expertise in arson, comes to her aid, but will it be in time to save her?

TRAPPED, Book Three
Second Chances. Cornered. Murder.

Sadie Williams receives a cryptic and terrifying call from her scared sister. But when Sadie arrives at her identical twin's home, there's no sign of Katie, only evidence of a quick flight. The puzzling situation turns potentially deadly when intruders storm the house. With help from Brock Carrington, her ex-fiancé and an ex-Marine, Sadie narrowly escapes.

Brock is an injured veteran dealing with PTSD. He's finally piecing his life back together when his ex-fiancée needs his help. Can Brock reignite their relationship and find her missing twin before they're both killed?

KIDNAPPED, Book Four
Abduction. Death. Second chances.

When Beth Sherman interrupts a break-in at her house, her life changes drastically. When K9 police officer, Colby Parker, returns to his hometown after years of staying away, he finally must face his feelings concerning the murder of his fiancée.

Circumstances throw Beth and Colby together when a person leaves bombs in different public places around Cimarron City. They both have given up on love, but caught up in the dangerous situation, the pair find themselves falling in love. But can it last, especially when Beth is kidnapped

Books in the
STRONG WOMEN, EXTRAORDINARY SITUATIONS
Series

DEADLY HUNT, Book One

All bodyguard Tess Miller wants is a vacation. But when a wounded stranger stumbles into her isolated cabin in the Arizona mountains, Tess becomes his lifeline. When Shane Burkhart opens his eyes, all he can focus on is his guardian angel leaning over him. And in the days to come he will need a guardian angel while being hunted by someone who wants him dead.

DEADLY INTENT, Book Two

Texas Ranger Sarah Osborn thought she would never see her high school sweetheart, Ian O'Leary, again. But fifteen years later, Ian, an ex-FBI agent, has someone targeting him, and she's assigned to the case. Can Sarah protect Ian and her heart?

DEADLY HOLIDAY, Book Three

Tory Caldwell witnesses a hit-and-run, but when the dead victim disappears from the scene, police doubt a crime has been committed. Tory is threatened when she keeps insisting she saw a man killed and the only one who believes her is her neighbor, Jordan Steele. Together, can they solve the mystery of the disappearing body and stay alive?

DEADLY COUNTDOWN, Book Four

Allie Martin, a widow, has a secret protector who manipulates her life without anyone knowing until...

When Remy Broussard, an injured police officer, returns to Port David, Louisiana to visit before his medical leave is over, he discovers his childhood friend, Allie Martin, is being stalked. As Remy protects Allie and tries to find her stalker, they realize their feelings go beyond friendship.

When the stalker is found, they begin to explore the deeper feelings they have for each other, only to have a more sinister threat come between them. Will Allie be able to save Remy before he dies at the hand of a maniac?

DEADLY NOEL, Book Five

Assistant DA, Kira Davis, convicted the wrong man—Gabriel Michaels, a single dad with a young daughter. When new evidence was brought forth, his conviction was overturned, and Gabriel returned home to his ranch to put his life back together. Although Gabriel is free, the murderer of his wife is still out there and resumes killing women. In a desperate alliance, Kira and Gabriel join forces to find the true identity of the person terrorizing their town. Will they be able to forgive the past and find the killer before it's too late?

DEADLY DOSE, Book Six
Drugs. Murder. Redemption.

When Jessie Michaels discovers a letter written to her by her deceased best friend, she is determined to find who murdered

Mary Lou, at first thought to be a victim of a serial killer by the police. Jessie's questions lead to an attempt on her life. The last man she wanted to come to her aid was Josh Morgan, who had been instrumental in her brother going to prison. Together they uncover a drug ring that puts them both in danger. Will Jessie and Josh find the killer? Love? Or will one of them fall victim to a DEADLY DOSE?

DEADLY LEGACY, Book Seven
Legacy of Secrets. Threats and Danger. Second Chances.

Down on her luck, single mom, Lacey St. John, believes her life has finally changed for the better when she receives an inheritance from a wealthy stranger. Her ancestral home she'd thought forever lost has been transformed into a lucrative bed and breakfast guaranteed to bring much-needed financial security. Her happiness is complete until strange happenings erode her sense of well being. When her life is threatened, she turns to neighbor, Sheriff Ryan McNeil, for help. He promises to solve the mystery of who's ruining her newfound peace of mind, but when her troubles escalate to the point that her every move leads to danger, she's unsure who to trust. Is the strong, capable neighbor she's falling for as amazing as he seems? Or could he be the man who wants her dead?

DEADLY NIGHT, SILENT NIGHT, Book Eight
Revenge. Sabotage. Second Chances.

Widow Rebecca Howard runs a successful store chain that is being targeted during the holiday season. Detective Alex Kincaid, best friends with Rebecca's twin brother, is investigating the hacking of the store's computer system. When the attacks become personal, Alex must find the assailant before Rebecca, the woman he's falling in love with, is murdered.

DEADLY FIRES, Book Nine
Second Chances. Revenge. Arson.

A saboteur targets Alexia Richards and her family company. As the incidents become more lethal, Alexia must depend on a former Delta Force soldier, Cole Knight, a man from her past that she loved. When their son died in a fire, their grief and anger drove them apart. Can Alexia and Cole work through their pain and join forces to find the person who wants her dead?

DEADLY SECRETS, Book Ten
Secrets. Murder. Reunion.

Sarah St. John, an FBI profiler, finally returns home after fifteen years for her niece's wedding. But in less than a day, Sarah's world is shattered when her niece is kidnapped the night before her vows. Sarah can't shake the feeling her own highly personal reason for leaving Hunter Davis at the altar is now playing out again in this nightmarish scene with her niece.

Sarah has to work with Detective Hunter Davis, her ex-fiancé, to find her niece before the young woman becomes the latest victim of a serial killer. Sarah must relive part of her past in order to assure there is a future for her niece and herself. Can Sarah and Hunter overcome their painful past and work together before the killer strikes again?

About the Author

Margaret Daley, a *USA Today* Bestselling author of over 105 books (five million plus sold worldwide), has been married for over forty-seven years and is a firm believer in romance and love. When she isn't traveling or being with her two granddaughters, she's writing love stories, often with a suspense/mystery thread and corralling her cats that think they rule her household. To find out more about Margaret visit her website at www.margaretdaley.com.

Facebook:
www.facebook.com/margaretdaleybooks

Twitter
twitter.com/margaretdaley

Goodreads
www.goodreads.com/author/
Margaret_Daley

Link to sign up for my newsletter on front page of website: www.margaretdaley.com